HOPE

Dynamism of a
Will and Way to Win

DR. GIDEON ADJEI

HOPE
Dynamism of a Will and Way to Win

ISBN (Paperback): 979-8-89672-195-6
ISBN (Hardback): 979-8-89672-197-0
ISBN (Ebook): 979-8-89672-196-3

PROMINENT
BOOKS
EDGE

5830 E 2nd St, Ste 7000 #9983
Casper, WY 82609
USA

Other Books by
DR. GIDEON ADJEI

Darker Shades of Light

Black Ice: A Vision for Victory

One Plus One Equals One: Secrets to the
Divine Plan for a Successful Marriage

Uno más Uno es Igual a Uno: Secretos del Plan Divino
Para Matrimonios Exitosos (Spanish Edition)
Breaking Through the Clouds of the Spirits of Jezebel

Rompiendo las Nubes de los Espíritus
de Jezabel (Spanish Edition)

DEDICATION

This book is dedicated to Yeshua of Nazareth

ACKNOWLEDGMENTS

I would like to thank my wife, Irene Adjei, for her love and support. Sincere thanks also go to Eugenia Pearl Quaye and Eva Doris Adjei for their encouragement. Family life is very important to me. Therefore, I would like to extend special thanks to our children Alvin, Vanessa, Crizia Joyce, and Arvin for cheering me on.

The author is deeply and sincerely grateful to Alvin Adjei, JD, for writing an insightful Preface to this book.

Special appreciation also goes to Rev. Stephen Deyo and Rev. Jazmine Deyo for the Foreword to this book.

ABOUT THE AUTHOR

D r. Gideon Adjei is a distinguished professor. He has a passion and talent for creative writing. He is the author of the following books: Darker Shades of Light, Black Ice: A Vision for Victory, One Plus One Equals One: Secrets of the Plan for a Successful Marriage (English and Spanish versions), and Breaking Through the Clouds of the Spirits of Jezebel (English and Spanish versions). After nearly two decades of writing mystery and romantic books, he has developed a unique writing style that piques the imagination of his audience. This attribute is exemplified by the tantalizing use of both conventional and spiritual principles by the principal character in his latest work, HOPE: Dynamism of a Will and Way to Win, to successfully rise above the storms of life in a dramatic and suspenseful way. Dr. Adjei was educated at Texas A&M University, Oklahoma State University, the University of Arizona, and the University of Houston. Among his other accomplishments, Dr. Adjei previously served as an international environmental consultant, prayer director for the Galveston and Houston markets of Family Life's Weekend to Remember marriage seminars. Family Life is a *Cru* Ministry. He was also the executive director of a charitable cross-cultural educational organization, Sankofa: A Global Reunion. Dr. Adjei resides in Houston, Texas. He is the presiding prelate of Adjei Ministries & Evangelistic Network (AMEN). His hobbies include reading, writing, traveling, and researching the secrets of longevity.

FOREWORD

Power of Hope in Our Weakest Moments

ope is one of the most powerful forces in the universe, and we are reminded of it and inspired with it by this book. It is in our weakest moments that having *hope* can uplift us the most. A hopeful person experiences life with faith and love, which empower them to overcome unexpected obstacles and eventually become victorious.

The testimony of the power of *hope* that I wish to share is that of my mother, Sandi Deyo. She was a person that stood for hope. Her Christlike love for others always inspired many, including myself. She was a chaser of dreams and lived an adventurous and joyful life. From a young age, she discovered her talent for singing and performing, and she loved to share her gift of voice to uplift people through music.

She was a loving mother to her two children, always a shoulder to lean on, and a compassionate friend. She was very charismatic and creative throughout her work as an entrepreneur. She launched several small businesses, including an electrical service business with her husband, and other times worked as a professional musician, vocal instructor, and fitness coach.

At the age of fifty, she was diagnosed with lymphoma cancer, but when faced with seemingly dark times, she drew on her faith in prayer to God and her inner strength to persevere. She kept a radiant smile on her face and focused on the positivity around her. Throughout the nine-year healing journey since her diagnosis, she befriended others in hospitals, clinics, healing centers, and churches who were facing terminal illnesses. She shared her testimony and positivity and gave hope to others who seemed hopeless through brotherly and sisterly love. She ministered and shared the gospel to people whom God placed on her path.

In her final weeks, she told me and my wife that she could see the presence of Yeshua himself. Her faith allowed her to see the Son of God at her bedside, coaching and comforting her as she performed physical therapies and as she slept at night. She sent our family this message: "I'll not give up. Yeshua is with me. I am Yeshua's. He has the only and the final word. The alpha and the omega. He always has me by his strong right hand and I feel him. With Yeshua as my coach, I stand victorious! I am a Victor!"

She lived a life of hopeful faith. Hope carried her through the effects of her illness, and hope carried her through the transition beyond this life.

Just like the main character in this book, *Hope*, Sandi also placed her absolute trust in God. The root of her healing was the peace she felt in the presence of God. Because she placed all of her faith in God, she achieved the ultimate victory.

During one of our last conversations, she asked me how I would know it was her when she appeared to me after she transitioned from this life. Then we both agreed I will know in my heart when it is her and I will feel a connection with her always. We ended that conversation with hope in the afterlife and hope to see each other again. After she passed, I had a dream where she appeared, and as we embraced, I said, "There you are," and she replied, "Here I am!" This spiritual vision of our meeting in a dream gives me hope.

May Sandi's testimony of *hope* energize and encourage others. May the reader of this book tap into the courage to draw from inner strength and determined willpower to remain hopeful through trials and tribulations until the ultimate victory. Amen

Rev. Stephen Deyo and Rev. Jazmine Deyo

CONTENTS

PREFACE

We live in an age where disinformation, depression, and distraction are the norm. The news is replete with information regarding the doom and gloom of a pending recession, senseless and randomized gun violence, or the resurgence of a global pandemic, to name a few. The impact and gravity of such information on the general population is enough to make you throw up your hands in exasperation.

Someone once said that life is not a destination but a journey. In these dark times, we could all benefit from a glimmer of hope that brings with it a certain amount of joy and insight to guide us in this slippery and seemingly uncertain journey.

This powerful fictional story, *HOPE: Dynamism of a Will and Way to Win*, is a book that nourishes and nurtures us and quenches our thirst for guidance to navigate the difficult journey of our times. In a thrilling, suspenseful, and mystical manner, the principal character of the story, Hope, exudes a variety of attributes. These unique qualities help him to circumvent the long odds and obstacles that stand between him and his divine destiny articulated by his earthly parents. He does so in a patient and clever manner that invokes our sympathy and identification with him.

When we first meet Hope, we find him in a happy setting. He resides with both parents in the haven of their stable and lovely home located in a well-to-do neighborhood. He is of the lineage of the founding fathers of the city of Avenice. However, early in the story we learn that the city of Avenice faces economic decadence due to mysterious political circumstances. His parents, inspired by love and faith, believe that he will rise to be a great man who will lead their city to economic prosperity and redeem their family name and prestige. In his early life, Hope continues to display natural leadership ability. He is well liked, smart, and hardworking. However, it is not too long before Hope's purpose is frustrated by the storms of life. Life strips him of the people closest to him. He loses his family, his reputation, and seemingly his future.

At the climax of the story, Hope feels downtrodden and depleted of options. He is in a difficult and seemingly unsurmountable situation. He sets out on a journey to an unknown destination. Over a period, his cognitive skills, coupled with life's experiences teach him that, if he is going to fulfill his purpose, he must answer seven questions:

1. What do we do when circumstances out of our control befall us?
2. How do we respond to the people who wrong us?
3. Why it is not justified to seek vengeance?
4. What can sustain us when we fall into the pit of life?
5. Where do we draw strength from to change our circumstances when everything around us makes us feel so powerless?
6. Does faith have any place in the realm of the living?
7. When one becomes a victor and not a victim of circumstances, why is it important to give credit to those that help us along the way?

The challenges Hope faces come upon him suddenly and sometimes mercilessly. Ultimately, Hope learns the lessons needed to fulfill his future. He discovers that prayer, forgiveness, justice, will, faith, humility, and lastly hope are the key to his success. The secret and mystical power of these seven attributes help to transform him from a life of loneliness and depression to one full of happiness and success. Join us to be entertained and inspired and to learn about how Hope overcomes the obstacles in his life. I hope that after reading this book filled with the rigor and relevance of hope for the future, you too will learn how to overcome the storms in your life to fulfill the destiny that is set before you.

Alvin Adjei, JD

Houston, Texas

Childhood Days

Edmund and Charlotte De Pinto had been married for ten years. Charlotte was much younger than Edmund. Edmund had inherited a good deal of wealth from his politically astute parents, who were of the lineage of the founding fathers of the city of Avenice. The city of Avenice enjoyed a booming economy and political power for many years.

A major contributor to its enviable socioeconomic standing was that it was home to a large naval airbase. Additionally, several aerospace engineering companies provided employment to its population.

In fact, Avenice enjoyed a formidable reputation as a swing district in key political elections.

Ten-thousand-foot high rocky mountains surrounded the city. A variety of lush vegetation covered these scenic mountains. Additionally, the mountain range made it a natural location for the storage of strategic intercontinental ballistic missiles. The Department of City Beautification maintained impeccable aesthetics for Avenice. Zoning laws were strictly enforced.

In the process of time, a new generation of younger inhabitants with alternate ideas from those of the founding fathers populated that rapidly growing city. Their political actions steered the city away from the conventional political wisdom of the founders.

All eyes were on the upcoming hotly contested presidential election during the fall of the year. Pollsters of the incumbent president who sought a second term in office determined that the citizens of Avenice leaned toward the views of the opposing candidate. His political strategists conceived and implemented numerous activities to sway the people of Avenice to the side of the incumbent presidential candidate. Voter turnout in Avenice was extremely high on the day of the election.

None of those corrective measures implemented by the incumbent's political strategists worked as they expected. Consequently, the incumbent lost his bid for a second term by a very narrow margin. He decided to do something about that situation before he left office.

Rumors around town suggested that the change in political atmosphere and voting pattern in Avenice had led to the suspicious closure of the naval air base, which was the economic lifeblood of the city. That sad and clandestine political maneuver had a significantly adverse economic impact on the city. The entire community was caught off guard by the sudden closure.

They soon realized that their once-thriving city was on the verge of going from boom to bust. Conversations in social media, as well as various places of mass gathering, focused on the dire need for the local government to take drastic measures to avert the dismal changes that were about to take place in the city.

The inhabitants cried foul to the suspected executive action of the outgoing president. However, there was nothing they could do to reverse it. With the resultant economic decline of Avenice, the wealth and political influence of the De Pinto family steadily waned.

Charlotte and Edmund suffered tremendous financial losses as a direct consequence of the economic downturn of their city. Most of their thriving businesses in the city soon went out of business. They struggled to hold on to what they could but to no avail. As time progressed, their financial losses took a toll on their marital relationship.

Yet the strong bond of love that had held their marriage together thus far kept them together. In their heart of hearts, they hoped that one day a charismatic person from within their family would arise, endowed with natural talents and abilities to bring about a change in the economic status of Avenice. They longed for a charismatic leader, endowed with the dynamism of a will and way to win back the prestige of their beloved city and their family's economic status and political power.

As the De Pinto family sat around the dinner table one Saturday afternoon, they watched a fiery speech by a motivational speaker. He cited examples of the timely arrival and impact of deliverers like Moses, Joseph, and Yeshua of Nazareth. Such leaders, he said, were previously unknown. Yet their timely arrival at the social arena made an enormous, indelible impact on the well-being of humanity. The De Pintos longed for someone strong, courageous, and imaginative enough to turn the economic status of Avenice around.

During those trying days, Charlotte found out that she was pregnant. Complications of pregnancy brought on frustrations, impatience, stress, and sometimes anxiety within the family. Nevertheless, the overwhelming faith they cherished that one day their progeny would rejuvenate the final flickering flames of economic prosperity for Avenice gave them hope for a better future together.

Charlotte's baby was due in April of that year. Edmund continued to display qualities of a responsible, supportive husband. For a man who used to be financially independent, he swallowed his pride and took on additional jobs to make ends meet for his family. Additionally, he made time to take Charlotte out for walks in the cooler evenings when he did not have to work.

Charlotte's delivery came on time, as predicted by her gynecologist. On April 13, she gave birth to a boy. The baby was a good eight-pounder with broad shoulders, round face, long fingers, and a head full of hair. He must have inherited his tresses from his mother.

Charlotte and Edmund received many compliments about the looks of their son. At an early age, he manifested gracefulness and charisma. They continued to entertain the hope that he might be a compelling leader one day. In light of their multilingual abilities and mixed ancestry, they named him L'Espoire, which means Hope.

Hope slept most of the night. There was something unusual about Hope. Though a baby, his actions and behavior indicated that he sensed his parents needed rest at night. When he woke up during the day, he stared at his mother's face, especially right in her eyes, and then smiled.

He sometimes woke up at night and seemed to expect to feel the warm and gratifying arms of his mother around him. When he did wake up during the late night hours, Charlotte sang a particular song to lull him back to sleep. Her mom had sung that same song to her when she was a baby. Hope was restless in the arms of other people. He was uniquely attached to his mother. Because of his close bond to his mother, some people thought he should have been born a girl instead of a boy!

By all accounts, Hope was treated like royalty despite the financial strain his family experienced. The De Pinto family continued to survive reasonably well on their reduced income. They ensured Hope had all he needed. Scarcely a day passed without someone stopping by to visit the young Hope.

As the days turned into weeks, and weeks to months, Hope was no longer a baby. He gradually grew to become a healthy boy. He had an unforgettable, vibrant look in his eyes that seemed to penetrate the hearts and souls of those around him.

Both Edmund and Charlotte continued to hold on to an inkling that Hope would one day fulfill their aspirations as the visionary leader Avenice needed to turn around their lives, as well as the economic decay of the city around them.

Hope learned to walk at an early age. With time, he became more and more relaxed in the presence of strangers. If someone just touched his cheeks, he would wear a broad smile on his face as if to say, "Thank you. I needed that." He picked up sounds and learned to pronounce certain words clearly at an early age.

Soon it was time for Hope to be registered for school. Both of his parents loved him and were very proud of him. They spoke positive words to encourage him always.

Just as he had learned to walk and talk much earlier than most kids his age, he also developed an interest in trying his hand at anything that looked challenging or curious. His parents thought that was an asset. Nevertheless, they kept a close watch on him to ensure he did not meddle with things that might harm him.

The De Pintos were health conscious. They incorporated a lot of fruit and fiber in their diet. They took strolls at the park regularly and loved to eat fresh foods. They did all that they could to avoid canned foods and preservatives. They additionally loved to make and drink smoothies rather than canned, acidic beverages. They were teetotalers who did not smoke.

Edmund loved gardening as a hobby. He sectioned off an area in their backyard to stockpile compost. Within that area, he grew vegetables of various kinds. Hope had watched his father pick up some greens in their backyard garden on several occasions. Later, Charlotte used the green vegetables harvested from that garden as delicious ingredients in their meal.

It so happened that Edmund had to work overtime periodically as they adjusted to life under the economic downturn of Avenice. That extra income came in handy to take care of some of their needs. Due to overtime demands from his job, Edmund now and then neglected to pull out certain weeds that cropped up among the desirable plants he cultivated.

DeAndria, Lovelle, Lasha, and Dick were Hope's neighborhood friends. They played with him from dawn to dusk, especially on weekends, until their parents called for them to come home for dinner. One warm summer afternoon, when Edmund was working overtime, as they played in the backyard of Hope's house, some of the weeds that grew in Edmund's garden caught their attention. Hope and his friends scrutinized one particular weed plant with variegated leaves. Hope told them how his dad harvested greens from the garden to be used as delicious ingredients in their dinners.

"Oh! Look at how the leaves match the spots in the flower petals," cried DeAndria.

"I wish I had that to decorate my birthday cake," Lovelle remarked.

"No, you can't have that," said Dick. "My mom said that we should not pick up any flowers or plants from the bush."

"You chicken!" retorted Lasha. "This is not the bush; this is Hope's father's garden! Smell it! Ah! It smells so sweet." Since Edmund was at work, the kids did not have an adult to talk to about the unique plants they saw in the garden. Aside from that, Charlotte had visitors. Consequently, the children could not interrupt her.

Hope quietly kept his comments to himself. Later that day, they played hide-and-seek. Hope hid under one of the shrubs his father had planted in their backyard. As he stayed in hiding all by himself, he recalled the various comments and suggestions of his friends about the plants in the garden. He wondered what would happen if he tasted some of the leaves raw instead of having them cooked.

He plucked off a few of the leaves, smelled them, and then threw them away. After a short while, he thought he heard a voice instruct him to pluck off some more leaves and taste them to satisfy his curiosity. They had a bitter taste. He focused on the leaves of one particular plant that had an appealing aromatic smell. He put a few of its leaves in his mouth, chewed them, and then swallowed them. They had a bittersweet taste. He gathered more leaves, rubbed them between his hands, and smelled them. Within seconds of exposure to the air, they developed a strong odor.

Unfortunately, this was a noxious, poisonous plant adapted to their region. Hope mistook it for an edible herb Edmund had harvested on previous occasions for their dinner.

While Hope experimented with the weeds in the garden, his friends sought him. Little did they know that he was in trouble—a lot of trouble. They eventually caught up with him. He appeared a little sluggish. Seeing that, they stopped for the day and went to their respective homes.

Later that night Hope felt feverish. He knew there was something wrong with him, but he was scared to tell his parents what he had done in the garden. He wanted to avoid getting a spanking. He grew restless and felt like vomiting.

Charlotte observed his restlessness and felt his high body temperature. She pressed him for answers. "What is wrong with you, son?. You look restless."

"Oh! Nothing. Just a little tired. I think I will feel better after I take a nap," he replied.

"No," she persisted, "you look pale. What were you doing with your friends in the garden? Tell me before it gets too late, my dear. Don't hide anything from me."

Hope felt like crying. He sensed that his mother was determined to get the truth out of him. He could no longer hide what had taken place in their backyard garden from her, and so he broke the bad news to her.

"Oh my gosh! Why didn't you tell me that earlier?" she demanded.

She immediately gave him a glass of milk and was about to call for an ambulance when Edmund walked in from work. Within minutes, Hope arrived at a nearby hospital. Fortunately, a pediatrician specializing in toxic substances was on special duty that night. He quickly diagnosed and administered the perfect antidote to Hope.

That pediatrician told Charlotte and Edmund that their timing in bringing Hope to the hospital was great. If they had waited a few additional minutes, the outcome would have been bad for him. Thank goodness, nothing fatal happened!

After that traumatic experience, Hope asked his parents to forgive him for hiding the truth of his experiments in their backyard garden. He promised he would never allow that to happen again. He was an introvert by nature. However, from then on he became a more cautious child. He did not experiment with things he had little knowledge of. He became more inquisitive and asked many questions about things he did not clearly understand in his surroundings.

His parents monitored his daily activities more closely than they had before. He learned a lesson. However, he had learned it the hard way. His parents did all they could to keep him happy as an only child. They bought him all the toys he asked for. They also observed that he seemed quite interested in using the wooden building blocks to build miniature houses. Thus, they assumed he might grow up to be an architect or engineer.

If their speculation was correct, then they hoped that their cherished dream for their only son to become the vessel through whom Avenice would regain its former prestige and economic status would materialize. They were aware that it would take patience, longevity, good health, time, money, and commitment to bring that to pass.

Whenever doubts lurked at the back of their minds, the fiery speech of the motivational speaker they heard who cited examples of Moses, Joseph, and Yeshua of Nazareth motivated them to remain hopeful and hold on to their dreams and aspirations for Hope's future accomplishments.

As they soon discovered, time can do a great deal. It would take faith for their dreams to materialize. The object of their faith must be in God in whose realm nothing is impossible. They would eventually learn that faithful believers in Him must undoubtedly submit their prayers and supplications to Him without wavering. If they did that, then they could expect answers to their prayers and supplications in accordance with His will. Similarly, they would also learn the power of forgiveness to any who had wrongfully treated them.

Fishing in Troubled Waters

Soon Avenice had lost most of its inhabitants faster than expected. Remarkably, however, it remained one of the cleanest cities one could find. Despite its economic difficulties, one could see the glittering sun shining over its irregularly shaped caldera lake with its adjoining streams to the north of the city.

One admired the striking greenness of the neatly mowed grasses along its roadways, as well as the scattered evergreen trees that provided abundant shade at various places within its city limits. Some of the most beautiful plants in the world grew in that area. The colorful variegated leaves of some of the plants in and around the city were a remarkable sight. Numerous insects wafted about, sucking nectar from the flowering plants.

Numerous species of birds seemed to have migrated from afar. It was a calming experience at dawn to watch the rhythmic reflection of the swelling sun on the clear bluish lakes to the east side of the city. Their elegant sparkle literally set that part of the city ablaze with unimaginable and mesmerizing scenic beauty. Many wondered why Avenice did not earn the accolade of "Sparkling City by the Lakes."

The De Pinto family were very educated. Prior to incorporating Avenice as a city, they ran the affairs of that town through family meetings. Such meetings were presided over by an immediate family member, chosen by acclamation.

During one of those meetings, the family made a business decision to develop and implement a conservation easement to protect and preserve the scenic and wildlife habitat attributes of the western parts of Avenice, including several caverns located along the western fringes of the city. Detailed reasons and justifications for such a legal document were drafted, voted on by the family representatives, and explicitly recorded in the original deed of conveyance, in perpetuity.

In a subsequent family meeting of the De Pinto family, Edmund's father, Bernard Timothy De Pinto, affectionately called B.T. by those who knew him well, made a startling modification to that deed. B.T. served as head of the De Pinto clan during that time. Those who closely interacted with him considered him a genius.

A trained attorney by profession, B.T. proposed a modification to the existing conservation easement. His modification granted a right to the easement holder, the local city government, to simply agree with the landowner (the De Pinto family) or their successors in interest to substantially modify or terminate the easement. That could be done whenever the holder, rather than a court, should determine that the stated purpose of that easement was either obsolete or impractical.

The implication of B.T.'s proposal was that the local government could at its discretion continue enforcing the easement or release some or all of the development and use restrictions in the easement in exchange for cash or other compensation.

The family members adopted and duly included that modification of the easement. However, for some reason no one paid much attention to it. All that was ingrained in the minds of the local government officials, and the city as a whole, was that no improvements were allowed within the western fringes of the city.

Avenice was located only a few miles from an ocean. Thus, its inhabitants had the choice of either freshwater or saltwater fishing.

Early one Saturday morning, the skies were clear and the winds low. Despite the deceptive calmness, the weather service issued an advisory against the use of small boats at sea. They expected rough weather at sea later that evening.

A similar weather bulletin issued the previous week had not turned out to be accurate. Mother Nature sometimes seems to have a mind of its own in such mysterious phenomena.

Edmund and his friends, Jerry, Mark, and Dino, sat under the shade of one of the fig trees in his house. They toyed with the idea of going fishing to get them out of the boredom, which characterized some Saturday afternoons in Avenice.

They envisioned the excitement of fishing in the nearby crystalline waters. It would be their first ever real fishing trip at sea. They had done some fishing on and off with some of their coworkers in the small lakes and adjoining rivers that surrounded the eastern parts of the city.

Jerry, the most experienced angler of them all, recounted stories about his experiences with deep-sea fishing. He mentioned a few incidents about what could be expected at sea, especially in rough weather. However, that did not deter them from carrying out their fishing plans. Aside from that, Jerry had bought a brand new forty-foot boat and was anxious to take it out at sea.

They checked and double-checked all that was necessary for their trip. Jerry's new boat was equipped with the latest citizen's band radio and life vests. They were convinced they had nothing to fear.

Charlotte tried unsuccessfully to talk Edmund out of that fishing trip. She thought the following weekend might be better. She was willing to accompany him if he agreed to postpone it. However, he insisted on hanging out with his friends that afternoon. Aside from that, he was convinced they might be back before the predicted change in the weather. Within minutes, the brave quartet were on their way to Kingcola Bay. Most of the fish they expected to catch were red fish, snappers, drum, kingfish, and bass.

As they prepared to launch Jerry's boat at Kingcola Bay, Edmund's discussion with Charlotte, which had almost turned into a hot argument, flashed in his mind. He had doubts whether he should have listened to his wife and stayed home with his family. Then he saw other people having fun at sea and saw no reason why they could not do the same. After all, he mused, life was what one made it to be, and one had only one life to live.

Suddenly, a thought struck him. Charlotte would be elated if he caught and brought home to her a giant kingfish, her favorite.

Hope had overheard the conversation of his parents about that fishing trip. However, he fell sound asleep when his father left to go fishing with his friends. Hope had a horrible dream about that fishing trip. He had the gift to see things in his dreams that eventually happened in reality. However, he was not mature enough to understand the significance of what he saw in his dream. He kept turning one way and then another in bed. Finally, he woke up crying.

"No, no, no," he screamed as he woke from his dream. Charlotte heard him scream and rushed immediately to his room. She asked Hope what was amiss, but he could not explain it to her. He asked for his dad with a tense look on his face.

Meanwhile, Edmund and his friends continued to have fun at sea. It apparently was a great day for fishing. Dino had the least experience fishing of the group. He kept using up the bait they took along with them. He caught no fish because he did not realize he must jerk the fishing pole when he felt the fish biting on the bait. Instead, he rolled the reel as soon as he felt the fish biting at the bait. Finally, Jerry gave Dino a lesson on the rudiments of deep-sea fishing. After that, he was able to reel them in one after the other.

After listening to Hope's dream, Charlotte felt it was a bad omen for Edmund and his friends at sea. She did her best to clear that off her mind but could not.

The seawater was so clear on that Saturday afternoon that one could actually see some of the fish coming to take a bite at the bait. Little did they know that that fishing trip had their doom written all over it!

They were so preoccupied with their fishing activity that they did not realize they had drifted thirty-five miles away from the shoreline. All around them, they only saw the deep blue waters of the sea but no other boats near them. It was as if they had the sea all to themselves.

They probably caught close to a thousand pounds of fish that day. Just as they were in the process of making that final catch, Edmund caught a forty-five-pound kingfish. He thought to himself that Charlotte would love that, after all.

Meanwhile, a deadly storm had built up at sea and was fast approaching them directly. The weather changed sooner than was expected. They should have paid heed to the weather advisory. Edmund in particular felt guilty he did not pay attention to Charlotte's plea for him to postpone that fishing trip. They sensed and felt the telling effects of the raging storm on their way back to shore.

The beautiful clear blue waters suddenly turned into raging, merciless rough waters. The sea waves shot higher than expected. It was obvious that their boat might capsize. Jerry tried to reach the coast guard but lost radio contact with them.

Thus, the first thrilling phases of deep-sea fishing excitement suddenly became the final flickering flames of dear life. Edmund saw in his mind's eye the conversation he had with Charlotte prior to their departure on that fishing trip. However, the old adage, "Had I known is always at last," proved once again to be true.

The roughness of the raging waves reached uncontrollable proportions, and suddenly the inevitable happened. The crew of another boat reported to the coast guard on safe arrival at shore that they left another boat several miles at sea and feared they were caught by the storm. The coast guard immediately sent specially equipped search and rescue boats to locate the missing anglers. Although the storm did not last too long, it was intense enough to give reason for suspicion, fear, and alarm.

The search crew rescued Jerry and Mark. A meticulous search by the coast guard for Edmund and Dino proved fruitless. The rescue team did not recover their bodies.

Charlotte faced dismal and negative feelings of loneliness due to the loss of her husband. Several of their family friends dropped by to express their sympathies and check on how well she and Hope were coping with their loss. The person who came by most frequently to visit was Beverly, a woman who had relocated to Avenice a year or so prior to Edmund's death under mysterious circumstances.

She was in her early forties. She had been divorced from her husband for almost eighteen months. Beverly was a talkative one, who could not keep any secrets. Edmund had cautioned Charlotte to keep her distance from Beverly. He thought she would be a bad influence on her. Aside from that, he did not want their personal business to get in the streets for all to know.

Actually, there was more to Beverly than Edmund wanted to share with Charlotte. Because of his family background, the late Edmund was privy to information that was tightly kept within closed circles. The concealed issue was that Beverly was a beautiful woman. However, her parents were very poor. Consequently, in her early teens they arranged for her to marry an older but wealthy man who had dubious business connections. With the passage of time, Beverly fell in love with her husband despite their significant age gap and shady business dealings.

She was not oblivious to the fact that such wealthy businesspersons were also womanizers. Despite that, Beverly continued in her jealous rages. Her husband spent several nights out presumably in the arms of other women. That became a bitter pill for her to swallow.

One day, in a jealous rage, she asked her chauffeur to take her to the house where he dropped off her husband. He refused. However, under constant assurance that she would protect the source of her information, he caved in.

He took Beverly close to her husband's mistress's house and knocked on the door. The mistress looked through the peephole and recognized Beverly. She went and informed her lover that his wife was at her front door. Surprised, he went to the door and asked Beverly how she knew where he was. One thing led to another. Ultimately, Beverly left and went home.

Next morning, the chauffeur went to pick up Beverly's husband. He asked the chauffeur about that incident which the chauffeur vehemently denied. The next day, Beverly's husband invited her to an evening out. He drove one of their many cars himself.

When Beverly asked why their chauffeur was not driving them, her husband smiled and told her he wanted her to see what happened to people who betrayed the trust of others. They stopped in front of a house at the outskirts of town. Two men greeted them and led them into a large upper room. There, Beverly saw the corpse of their chauffeur hanging from the ceiling. He had several bruises on his lifeless body.

Terrified, she screamed and cried her heart out on their way back home. At that moment, she made up her mind to escape from her husband. Through a series of complex events, Beverly eventually connected with an agency that looked for her husband.

In exchange for information that led to his arrest, that agency would place her in protective custody, give her a new identity, and subsequently relocate her to a place of safety to start a new life altogether. That was the way it was. No one including Beverly worried about her husband any longer. She ended up in Avenice under those circumstances. Edmund kept that top secret from Charlotte.

However, after Edmund's death Charlotte felt she needed a confidant. Someone with whom she could share her loneliness and frustrations. Someone who would give her support and encouragement. Since Beverly came by so often, she found it appropriate and convenient to discuss her personal matters with her. Soon, the two became close friends.

Charlotte had been born in a small country town only a few miles away from Avenice. As an only child, she knew no other world apart from that of her immediate family. She had a sheltered life while growing up. She did not have the opportunity to befriend others, as she would have liked to. Therefore, she did not really understand the behavior of people.

Edmund was older than she was. She wanted to have a father figure to continue steering her. Rumors had it that she was a virgin at the time of her marriage to Edmund. As such, he was both a best friend, lover, and father figure to her.

One Friday afternoon, Charlotte took Hope to one of the city parks. They watched the other kids play. Hope had memories of his late dad each time he saw another child of his age taking a stroll along the walkways at the park or playing with their dad. At one point Hope got thirsty. He walked to a nearby water fountain a few yards away from where they sat. Charlotte asked if he wanted her to walk him to the water fountain, but he said he wanted to go by himself.

On his way back from the water fountain Hope saw a bunch of kids on the swing sets at the park. One of them saw Hope as he walked by himself to rejoin his mother. He hollered for him to come and join them. At first, Hope was reluctant to join them. However, as the other kids in that group pressed him harder, he obliged.

It was his first time to ride a swing at the park. He really enjoyed that experience. So pleasant an experience it was for him that he virtually forgot that his mother was waiting for him at the spot where they shared a seat.

Before too long, a boy about five years older than Hope appeared on the scene. He was the elder brother of the one who first invited Hope to join them on the swing.

Incidentally, that boy was a notorious troublemaker among friends of his younger brother's.

For some reason, he gave each of the kids on the swing a hard push. At first it went well for those he pushed. However, when he got to Hope, he pushed him so hard that Hope was scared. In fact, Hope thought he was going to fall off the swing, and he screamed. The other kids looked on in dismay, except the big bully who stood by with a wry look on his face and then laughed at his folly.

When the swing slowed down, Hope got off. He walked boldly to the older boy to express his displeasure. As he walked away back to his mother, the person followed, and asked if he thought he was better than the rest of them. Since Hope ignored him, he got infuriated. He grabbed Hope by his shirt and challenged him to a duel. Hope asked him to let him go because he did not want to fight him. However, the bully was relentless and kept pushing on Hope. A struggle ensued as Hope tried to free himself.

Meanwhile Charlotte heard the commotion and run to rescue Hope from that bully. Before she got there, a man, who had come to the park with his daughter, outran her and separated the scuffling kids. "Is that your son," he asked Charlotte as she eventually arrived on the scene.

"Yes, he is my only son. Thanks for getting him out of the claws of this monster kid," she replied.

"What happened, son?" she asked Hope.

Hope recounted the incident in the presence of the man who had stopped it. The man took advantage of that opportunity to introduce himself and his daughter. He invited Hope to come over and play with his daughter so that he was out of the way of the other kids. However, in light of events, Charlotte decided to take her son home by cab instead.

The man gave his business card to Charlotte and offered that whenever Hope needed a friend to play with, his daughter was available. Charlotte thanked him for his kind offer and went home with her son.

School Days

Charlotte received a modest insurance claim because of her husband's accidental death. However, that depleted rapidly since she did not have supplemental insurance or part-time work. All her marital life she depended on Edmund, who was the breadwinner of his family. Edmund had depleted his inheritance due to their lavish lifestyle, business or investment losses, and downturn of the local economy.

As a token of recognition for the outstanding contributions they had made to Avenice, some members of the community organized fund-raisers. They gave the proceeds to Charlotte. She was very appreciative of that gesture, more so because it was time for Hope to begin elementary school.

Throughout his nursery and kindergarten years, Hope displayed encouraging learning abilities. His teachers found him to be a likable kid. Charlotte meticulously helped him with his work assignments. However, since she had only completed the seventh grade, she realized that Hope needed the services of a private tutor if he was to maintain excellent grades at school. However, she could not afford that.

Despite the odds against him. Hope did his best to keep up with his grades. He went on to junior high school. He consistently made the dean's list throughout his junior high school career. Everyone who saw his report cards were proud of him. He had very little interest in outdoor activities. He had a curious mind. His near-death experience had prepared him to always ask questions about issues or topics on which he had little knowledge. Oh, what a brilliant and ambitious chap!

His mother helped shape his image and perception of life. She encouraged him to follow his dream. Charlotte taught him that most successful people attained great heights in their lifetime by asking questions, performing experiments, and using both inductive and deductive reasoning to get answers to questions that were of interest to them.

As Hope attained manhood, he took on most of his late father's physical characteristics and habits. That reminded Charlotte of the days she had spent with Edmund. They were very memorable days, but she was reluctant to submit to the concept of predestination, though occasionally she was tempted to.

Then came the big moment. Hope gained admission to a prestigious high school. It was a boarding school. Charlotte was emotional to see Hope reach adulthood. Hope was flabbergasted that within a few short weeks he would enroll in a newly built high school in Avenice. He could not get over the readjustments he would have to make. The fear of the unknown stared him in the face—new friends, teachers, and food.

Charlotte used the donations she received from the Avenice community wisely. She sold a parcel of land that Edmund had acquired as an investment property. Each week she bought new clothing and other necessary items for her son. She believed the decision to send Hope to a boarding school was the correct decision rather than having to stay at home to attend a day school. Such an experience would make him more independent and better prepare him for the future, she thought.

The night before Hope left for his new school, all his neighborhood friends gathered at the De Pinto home to give him a final farewell. It was a very proud moment for him because based on his class record and exquisite score on the entrance examination, Hope was the only pupil who qualified for the newly established and heavily contested statewide A and A Foundation scholarship from his school district. That was a remarkable accomplishment.

He was tense and restless that night. He had mixed thoughts and feelings, and wondered what he might do to make his mother proud of him. He would miss their pet parrot, Spookier, and wondered what to say to the lone bird who had kept them company all those years.

He also wondered how the little girl next door, Angie, whom he had grown fond of, would take his departure from the neighborhood, at least for a few months at a time. Slowly but surely, Hope gave in to the overpowering demands of nature on human bodies. Before long, he was fast asleep.

The first person to show up at the front door to Hope's house was Angie. She wanted to wish him a second goodbye before he left. In fact, she asked to accompany Hope to school. After everything was taken care of, Charlotte drove Hope to his new school, and stayed with him until his registration was completed.

It was time for Charlotte and Angie to face the reality of the situation. They must leave Hope behind and return home. This would be the first time for Hope to spend the night away from home.

Mother and son had a very lengthy and affectionate conversation together before they parted. Charlotte in the end focused mostly on self-discipline and obedience. Finally, she told Hope, "My darling son, you know how much I love and cherish you. For a while, you will be on your own without me physically present with you. There are people here like you, some younger, and others older. Be careful whom you befriend. Do not deviate from your objectives. Always remember: whatever you do, my whole heart is with you, and heaven will help you if you help yourself." After those emotional words, she kissed him goodbye and walked away with teary eyes.

After completing his first year of life at that boarding school, Hope expressed his dissatisfaction with his new environment and teachers. He wished to transfer to another school. After carefully considering his request, Charlotte decided that her son's happiness at school far outweighed the prestige and scholarship of a brand-new school.

It turned out that when one door closes, another opens with new opportunities that are not immediately apparent. Appropriate transfer documents were completed, and Hope did not have to give up his A and A Foundation scholarship after all. An older boarding high school located close to the western fringes of the city admitted him. His great-grandfather had attended that school.

The night before his new school reopened, Hope slept soundly. He had a dream in which he stood at a place adjacent to a partially completed chapel. That chapel had a huge oak tree in front of it. In the dream he saw his late father with two other fellows in glistening attire and what appeared to be hard hats. They hovered over seven mountain peaks along the western fringes of Avenice. However, the closer he looked, he realized that hard hats were golden crowns.

Hope further observed that the crown worn by his father shone brighter than the other two. In the span of a moment, the seven mountain peaks where they stood compressed instantaneously into a white ball of fire that twisted into a horseshoe-like shape. As he drew closer to visualize the images in his dream, he suddenly woke up.

He wondered what that dream, apparition, or spiritual visitation might mean, especially in light of the fact that the founders of Avenice had a conservation easement in place that prohibited improvements in the western fringes of Avenice in perpetuity.

Though he was a young man, he was intuitive enough to have an awareness that there was something unusual about him. He was spiritually sensitive. Though he did not share that vision with anyone, he committed it deep into his long-term memory. He nurtured and savored it as a guiding light to his purpose on earth.

Shortly thereafter, the large antique wall clock in the hallway hanging on the eastern wall of their family room chimed the wakeup call. They got ready to leave for school one more time, accompanied by his mother. The first week at the school was solely devoted to orientation activities. It allowed the newer students to familiarize themselves with the campus and other related fields of interest.

Through that transitional period, Hope's mind was on nothing but home. He called his mother more than ten times during that week to inform her of his well-being. Certainly, they both missed each other.

His first day in class was quite an experience for him, to say the least. The students in his class were greatly diversified. They introduced themselves individually. Hope did not find a particular person he would befriend in class. He felt somewhat lonely and out of place.

That weekend, Charlotte and Angie came by to pay him a visit. "Tell me, how had everything been going with you, son?" asked Charlotte.

"I don't know yet," he replied. "However, I guess I will get used to the situation around here after a while. I do not want to bounce around like a rolling stone; can't gather any moss that way."

"I brought Angie with me," said Charlotte. "I thought it might be good for the two of you to chat face-to-face, and you could show her around while I visit with your counselor."

Angie and Hope got into a conversation. Neither of them had had new experiences with friendships. They missed each other very much. Hope shared his new experience on campus with Angie. He could not wait to get home to be with her as soon as school was over.

They took a long walk across campus. Angie admired their campus. Though it was located close to the western fringes of Avenice, she had never had reason to visit that campus. She looked forward to enrolling at that school the following year.

Hope noted that Angie's hair had grown longer, and her female features had become more distinct. He admired her even more and told her how pretty she had become. She reciprocated by complementing him on how masculine and handsome he had grown with the past few months. "Do you really like my hairstyle?" she asked.

"I guess you know by now that I sincerely do. I wish you would grow it a little longer. I have a thing about long hair," he replied.

"Well, how long is long?"

"I really don't know. I guess just long enough for you to be able to take good care of it. Keep that shine on it. I really,

really like that!" he exclaimed with a promising smile on his face.

No sooner had they gotten through with their intimate conversation than they saw Charlotte waving at them from beside a giant oak tree in front of Hope's dormitory. It was time for them to part company one more time. Hope kissed Angie on the cheek, as the day seemed to fly away like a beautiful dream.

The dullness of life on the campus motivated Hope to develop a great deal of interest in outdoor activities. His classes were over by three p.m. Between or after classes he made time to shoot pool and play ping-pong, softball, or handball or go swimming. In the evening, he consistently followed his study table and did all his homework and other assignments on time or watched TV at the student lounge.

He certainly created a perception in the mind of his instructors as an intelligent imaginative, responsible, and well-organized student. Additionally he showed traits of leadership and creativity. His counselor, Mr. Eddie Taylor, predicted he would be a great politician one day.

Hope had himself confided his intensions to be a senator or president. That was in line with the expectations of his parents. Hope was slated to complete his high school education right where he was. With the passage of time, he got into his final year.

The Party

The high school Hope attended was for boys only. The teachers at that institution were strict disciplinarians. There were amenities on-campus students could employ to while away the time after formal classes for those who wanted to. They placed strong emphasis on the rigor and relevance of student academic prowess.

That was the campus culture. It was a place for certain people to thrive and do well. While some students considered that campus life as antediluvian, characterized by "books and boredom," the campus administration continued that culture because several distinguished academic laureates elsewhere in the nation had completed their high school careers there.

Dick and Mickey were roommates who stayed across the hallway from Hope. Outwardly, they always appeared happy and satisfied. Their cheerful attitude caught Hope's attention. He made it a point to determine the secret of their happiness and satisfaction while others complained of boredom.

One Saturday morning as Hope took his shower in the common bathhouse, he overheard a conversation between Dick and Mickey. Mickey was attending nature's call while Dick smoked a cigarette, pacing up and down in the bathhouse.

"You've got to be on time, fellow," said Dick. "No lateness this time. I sure do not want to miss the first part of the party. We got there too late the other day."

"Well, man, I tell you what," Mickey responded. "We're going in my car today, and I'm leaving here at six on the dot."

"No, you aren't," growled Dick. "Have you forgotten that your radiator is leaking? That could blow up your motor, you know. Also, the last time we went over there, you got a speeding ticket from the highway patrol, and you have not paid that yet. You don't want to go to jail, do you? That means I'm driving."

"Well it is your car, man. We'll do it your way."

Hope tried to figure out the gist of their conversation. *Have I been missing something all the time I've been enrolled here?*

Melon City, a smaller town not far from Avenice, had a girls' vocational school. The students there were mostly high school dropouts. Once a month the school sponsored an entertainment gathering for the students. Only friends and acquaintances were invited. No overnight guests were allowed on the premises. One of those parties would take place at seven that evening.

Hope returned to his room to get dressed up. His curiosity about the brief conversation kept him restless. Thus, for once, he decided to show a little bit of inquisitiveness to his dormitory associates. He took the initiative to knock on their door.

"Who is it?" Dick asked.

"Hey, man, its Hope," he replied.

"Come on in, bookworm. What's on your mind?" Mickey asked as he swung the door open.

"I overheard your conversation in the bathhouse about a party this evening at seven p.m. I just wanted to know what you know that I do not know," retorted Hope.

Dick gazed at Mickey with a suspicious look on his face. They were not sure whether it would be a good idea to get Hope on board with them. They wondered what might happen to them if Hope found out what they really did at the party and squealed. On second thought, they took a chance and let him in on their secret adventures at that vocational school.

"Sounds exciting," Hope responded. "I think a slight change in environment might lift my spirits. Can I come with you guys?"

"No. However, if you cut a deal with us, we might be able to work out something," replied Mickey.

"What kind of a deal did you have in mind?"

"A very simple and straightforward deal. Nothing beyond your control," said Dick.

"Spell it out, guys. Let me hear it so that I will know if I can do it or not."

"Mickey and I have a math homework to do. The deadline for submission is by seven a.m. on Monday. However, we cannot miss this party. We have not been able to figure how to complete that assignment. However, a little bird tells us you are almost a genius when it comes to math."

"Here is the deal," said Mickey. "We will take you to the party if you agree to help us with the math assignment tomorrow night."

"You've got a deal," Hope agreed.

"Well, well, well, my man. At six p.m. tonight, meet us at Parking Lot E7," Dick concluded. Clearly this was a planned thing.

The trio left for Melon City at six p.m. straight up. A crowd had already gathered by the time they got to their destination. One could hear loud music being played by the disc jockey. No alcoholic beverages were served. Therefore, most of the invited guests who were familiar with the party rules stopped at liquor stores on their way to the party and bought small pocket-size bottles of booze, which they hid in their pockets.

Hope was bashful at that party. While the rest took to the floor, he stood by and watched them dance. He was not a good dancer. In fact, he had never attended a party of that magnitude.

One of the young ladies watching Hope as he stood alone boldly walked up to him and asked him a for a dance. Hope virtually refused to get on the dance floor. However, Dick and Mickey gave him a look. As a result, he obliged and danced with her.

After the music was over, his companions approached and asked him to get involved; otherwise, this would be the last time they would take him out with them.

Suddenly, the two girls who danced with Dick and Mickey gave them a signal. Hope did not know what that signal meant. In order not to offend his companions he accompanied them. One by one, they left and went behind the main hall where the party was organized.

One of the girls opened her purse and brought out a whole fifth of gin. How she got that, heaven only knew. They took sips of the gin and passed it around their group. Hope had to sip an alcoholic beverage for the very first time. He tried to wiggle his way out of drinking it. Then he saw the stern look on the faces of Dick and Mickey. Since he did not wish to offend them, he sipped about a mouthful of the stuff.

"Come on, man. You are a chicken. You have to be a man if you want to run with us," said one of the girls to Hope.

"Hey, don't bother this holy young man. He is going to spend eternity in heaven. But we are earthbound," said the other girl mockingly.

"Swell, what is an angel doing with us here in the first place?" Dick remarked. "He could have stayed in that boring dorm, and read his Bible."

Under such pressure from his companions, Hope sipped the hard liquor each time they passed it on to him. After a few such sips, it was evident he had gone past his tolerance level.

The adventurous group subsequently rejoined the rest of the crowd. Hope was very dizzy. He was tired and light-headed. He could not walk straight. In fact, it was difficult for him to stand still at one place. At one point, he fell to the floor and threw up. He was not fully aware of the big mess he had created. Oblivious, he was only trying to please his companions, who were used to tasting hard liquor.

Dick and Mickey rushed to his aid. They dragged him along the floor to a nearby bathroom. They ran some cold water over his head. They tried to give him an antacid to see if that would neutralize the alcohol, but Hope was so drunk that he could not open his mouth to take it.

Consequently, they left the party to take Hope back to the dormitory to sleep off the alcohol and get refreshed. He woke up the next day with a hangover. Dick and Mickey brought him some food from the canteen He slept the rest of the day. After that experience, he vowed to never drink again.

Uncovering the Empty Voids

Charlotte coped with Edmund's passing as much as she humanly could. However, loss of a spouse was not an experience one could easily dismiss. Edmund was a supportive husband. He always made her feel very special. She depended on his advice. He provided her a warm shoulder on which to cry. He entertained and showered her with gifts during their marital life.

Never a day passed by without him telling her how beautiful she looked. He spent time with her as she prepared meals. During the heyday of their marriage, Edmund took her out on cruises and short getaways to rekindle their relationship. Suddenly, he was no longer around to support or encourage her or give her that feeling of care and protection that she valued so much.

Compounding Charlotte's physical and emotional losses, Hope pursued his education away from home. Charlotte preoccupied herself with several activities meant to help her overcome the loss of her husband. Many a day, she complained of feeling both drained and tired, even though she did no exhausting work out of the ordinary. Though her finances were below what they used to be when her husband was alive, she managed to spend time at the malls shopping for various items on sale.

She engaged herself in taking long warm showers and often remained glued in front of the TV watching a variety of shows. Though she spent a significant amount of time on social media, joined several support groups, and sought help from family therapists and religious groups, her life was never the same.

She woke up sluggishly early one Monday morning but did not feel like getting out of bed. She'd had a very restless night. She pondered about other things she might do to help herself to overcome her loneliness. Then suddenly, a possible solution occurred to her. Though the prospects appeared grim, she must look for a job in town. She was convinced that if she successfully landed a job she had passion for and concentrated on it, she might better be able to break her preoccupation with thoughts about Edmund.

Aside from that, any additional income she derived would improve her financial predicament. She mused about the long-term impact of her decision might have on her current and future lifestyle, as well as her parental relationship with Hope.

Suddenly, Charlotte heard something drop at her front door. She got out of bed to investigate what she heard. It was the *Avenice Herald*. Edmund had subscribed to that local newspaper when he was alive. She wondered whether that was an omen from Edmund that confirmed her decision to look for work. Hitherto, she would have turned to the crossword puzzle page.

However, times had changed. Instead, she eagerly turned to the employment section, which she never bothered to peruse when her husband was alive. The employment listings were very brief. Nevertheless, that did not discourage her. Somehow, she felt a deep presence of her late husband around her.

Toward the bottom of the list of job openings, she saw the announcement for openings at a newly established textile plant on the outskirts of Avenice. She felt deep within herself that it might be worthwhile to pursue employment opportunities at that plant. Certainly several people would vie for that opportunity because of the downturn in the local economy.

She gave Beverly a call to share her decision with her and to solicit her opinions about that matter. She would be the one to transport her back and forth to work. Before she could reach the phone, it began to ring.

Coincidentally, Beverly was calling to gossip about what she and her boyfriend had discussed about Charlotte's situation. They thought it would help if Charlotte got a part-time job. Beverly's boyfriend had also heard about a small textile plant that was supposed to relocate to Avenice.

That meant there was a glimmer of hope for Charlotte to secure one of the positions that might be available. That was music to her ears. A telepathic connection between the late Edmund, Beverly, and her boyfriend and her. No, no, no. This could not have been a mere coincidence.

As expected, Beverly offered to give her a ride to her potential place of employment. In fact, Beverly considered employment at that same plant since she was dissatisfied with her current employer. Aside from that, it was rumored that that company had a reputation for paying high wages for its employees. Without further delay, the two friends were ready to go job hunting.

When they got to the plant site, they saw a long line of people awaiting their turn to be interviewed. As if by divine intervention, both Charlotte and Beverly were offered positions at the plant. Beverly immediately accepted the offer made to her because it was higher than what she currently made.

They were scheduled to undergo a short in-house training prior to starting their full-time positions with the company. They returned home and were elated at the good news they had received that morning. Beverly did not stay at Charlotte's residence too long. They both deserved a nap to rejuvenate from their surprise accomplishment that morning.

After a restful nap, Charlotte sat in the reclining chair her deceased husband used to occupy, especially on weekends when he watched football games. She had a vivid but brief dream about Edmund during her nap. In that dream she saw the two of them walking along a meandering trail adjacent to one of the clear crystal streams at the eastern fringes of Avenice.

They eventually came to a fork where they had to make a choice between making a left or right turn in order to get to their destination. Edmund pointed to the right fork. After they strolled for a few short yards in that direction, they saw an image that looked like the rising sun in the distant sky. Charlotte reached out her right hand to give Edmund a pat on the back. She could not but instead woke up from her dream.

She was hungry and craved for some seafood gumbo. It had been quite a long time since she had prepared such a meal. Yes, it was tricky to make a meal for one. She could not find the old recipe book her mother gave her when she got married. Thus, she closed her eyes and thought hard to remember as much of the recipe as she could.

As she began to prepare the meal, she amazingly recalled some of the ingredients the meal required. She looked through her pantry and deep freezer in the garage. She found some peeled shrimp she had bought at the farmers market a few weeks previously. She also found some butter.

She washed and added the butter to the shrimp and allowed it to cook until it turned pinkish. She next remembered to add some broth, flour, and oil and stirred the mixture. She was not one who measured ingredients whenever she cooked. She simply threw the items needed in the pot, stirred, and allowed them to simmer.

Then came the time to add additional items such as green bell peppers, garlic, onions, celery, thyme, rosemary, curry powder, and a weak alcoholic beverage. Finally, the remaining items came to her mind. Information that was committed from her short- to long-term memory. They included green onion, parsley, crabmeat, and finally a bowl of brown rice. Unbelievably, her seafood gumbo turned out delicious.

Later on that day, she called Hope and broke the news of her activities at home to him. He was quite satisfied with the reality that his dear mom had gained employment. She had never had to work in her entire life.

Privately, he cherished the idea that Charlotte could finally afford to buy him a bike he longed for and maybe a used car for him to cruise around in town whenever he came home on vacation, just like some of his affluent friends at school.

They had a very lengthy conversation—much longer than usual. Actually, Charlotte informed Hope that she had cell phones with unlimited calls and text messaging on her list of things to buy systematically, as she was paid.

At the end of their conversation, Charlotte told Hope, "Well, darling. I have to get off this phone. Mommy will be working hard to take better care of you. Don't you ever forget who you are and what we expect of you. Your ancestors founded this dying town. My dear son, continue to study hard so that you can become somebody one day and rescue this town from its economic decadence. Do not ever forget that. You know Mommy will always love you," said Charlotte.

I will, Mom, I will. You have nothing to worry about." replied Hope.

"And please stay away from bad company," she said softly. "Several young men with a lot of potential have wrecked their future through bad influence from others." She ended almost in tears.

"I will remember that," replied Hope. "Maybe I will grow up and become successful, and then marry into a rich family, and you won't have to work."

"You might as well forget about that. There are not any rich families around here any longer. With an educated mind you can reach unimaginable heights. Do not let anyone or anything stand in your way until you have achieved your goals. There is a lot at stake here. The hard work put in by your forefathers to establish this town, our family prestige, and the prosperity and happiness of the entire community are hanging on your shoulders," she added emotionally.

"I will do my best. That is a promise. As I said, you have nothing to worry about. It is a matter of time."

"Yes, son. In addition, time can do so much. Okay, bye, and I love you very much," she said.

"I love you too, Mom. Bye," responded Hope as he hung up the phone.

Since none of her TV shows played that night, Charlotte went to bed early in order to have enough rest for the next day's housekeeping she needed to do.

Hope came home occasionally on weekends. On one such occasion he and his mother were bored. They had stayed inside the house almost all day and thought about going to the movies. It had been quite a while since they last had such an outing. No sooner had they begun to get dressed for the theater than they heard someone knocking at their front door.

"Who is it?" Charlotte inquired

"It's me" was the reply.

"Me who?" Charlotte asked again.

"Beverly, it's Beverly. Please open the door."

Charlotte opened the door. To her surprise, Beverly was all dressed up and in good spirits.

"Where are you coming from, girl?" Charlotte asked. "You are dressed to kill."

"You look nice yourself," Beverly said. "I just stopped by to check on you two. I have a big idea. Won't it be nice for the three of us to do something for a change? The two of you have been indoors all day. How about the movies? Tonight I kind of feel bored."

"Why did you not call to inform us about that?" responded Charlotte. "Hope and I were thinking the same way. Actually, we were getting dressed to go see a movie playing at the Oxford. It has been the talk of the town lately."

"Like they say, when two testimonies agree, then that testimony is true. The Oxford is okay. However, I had in mind for us to go to the Orion," suggested Beverly. "*Kiddie's Baby* is playing. The story line I heard from people who went to see it means a lot to me."

Charlotte turned to Hope and asked for his opinion about Beverly's suggestion. To her surprise, Hope was flabbergasted with the apparent telepathic connection between the three of them. Aside from that, the Orion was the largest movie house in Avenice, and Hope privately entertained the idea that he would run into some of his friends there.

"To the Orion, then, we shall go. *Kiddie's Baby*, here we come," Beverly agreed.

The three of them left for the Orion at about 8:30 p.m. It was just about a twenty-minute drive away, so they could get there on time before the movie started. The Orion was fully packed. It was a sellout movie that night. If they had delayed a few minutes before they left home, they would have had difficulty getting in.

The show began at nine p.m. *Kiddie's Baby* was a story about the life of an attractive young woman who was the progeny of a mixed relationship. Her parents struggled financially to make ends meet. Consequently, they subjugated her in a sheltered life for most of her young adult years.

While in high school, she fell in love with a handsome young man from an affluent family enrolled in the gifted and talented class with her. Many people felt they would get married eventually. In the course of time, he enlisted into the army. Shortly thereafter, he was assigned to fight in a war-torn country overseas.

As the war dragged on, the young woman became increasingly lonely. Eventually, she was introduced to another handsome fellow from a far country who pursued a professional degree at a local institution. After almost three years of a sizzling romantic and promising potential for marriage, her original high school sweetheart returned home from his tour of duty.

A series of events culminated in the young woman falling back in love all over again with her original boyfriend. She reflected on how her parents had deprived her of social life and her frustrations about not being able to get the finer things in life like her friends and the freedom to live her young adult years normally.

Faced with that much frustration and financial burdens, she decided that marriage to someone from an affluent home, who had experienced discipline and survived a war, would be her way out of misery. Thus, she decided to get married at an early age to get away from home.

After several twists and turns in her married life, things shaped up for the better. She jilted her current boyfriend who had kept her happy and romantically satisfied and married her original high school sweetheart in pursuit of greener pastures.

In time, marital issues arose which at times were very intense. In one such episode, she left their house in a rage to take shelter and consolation with her parents as she had done on a few occasions.

She was involved in an accident with an eighteen-wheeler, whose driver was determined to be at fault. After a very sizable insurance settlement that some, especially her financially distraught parents, thought might bring happiness and peace to their home, their marital issues continued.

To further complicate matters, she was diagnosed with multiple sclerosis. That crippling disease progressed gradually until at times when she fell, she could not get back up unless her husband helped her.

Slowly but surely, her husband's true colors showed up. He was a bona fide womanizer. In fact, there were times when he brought different women to their house. He would intentionally push his wife down on the floor. While she helplessly remained on the carpet, unable to get up or reach the phone for help, he engaged in romantic episodes with his heartless girlfriends.

Such cruel, stressful experiences unleashed pronounced and excruciating pain on her. Her disease progressed rapidly to the point where he put her in a nursing home, she became completely paralyzed. However, she could at times speak audibly with great difficulty.

While in the nursing home, she recalled with regret why she jilted her other boyfriend, who had completed his education, single and was at the peak of his professional career.

She unsuccessfully tried to get in touch with him to apologize for what she did to him. Obviously, she knew the end was near for her. Eventually, a judge's wife who had an organization that reunited people heard about that woman's plight and took up her case. In her search, she came across the brother of the former boyfriend the woman wished to get in touch with. She rendered her apology and passed away shortly thereafter.

Charlotte watched that movie with undivided attention. Beverly had a surprising look on her face. Never in her association had she seen Charlotte so intensely engrossed in a social event as she was that night.

Charlotte felt restless as the movie ended. She remained glued to her seat as if she wanted to watch it all over again.

"Let's get going. Everyone's leaving us behind," noted Beverly.

To her surprise, Charlotte did not respond to her observation. She slowly got up and went through the walkway between the aisles out of the movie house.

"What's wrong, Charlotte? It appears to me you did not enjoy the movie. If it was the wrong choice, I must apologize."

"I guess it was all right. It gave me a lot to think about," she replied.

"What do you mean?" Beverly curiously asked.

"Well, a whole lot. I don't think I would like to talk about that now. All I feel like doing is getting home and catching up on my sleep," said Charlotte.

"Was there a particular scene that had a special significant impact on you?" inquired Beverly again.

"The entire movie," replied Charlotte. "The whole movie. I … I just don't know. Let's not talk about that right now, please." They got into Beverly's car and drove back home.

On her way back home after she dropped off Charlotte and Hope at their house, Beverly continued to ponder the change in Charlotte's attitude during and after the movie. She did not come up with a plausible reason for her friend's behavior. For that reason, she gave up on stressing herself out for an explanation.

However, that did not last for too long. She was a nosy person by nature, a die-hard who never gave up so easily. Naturally, she intended to pursue the matter succinctly the following day.

Charlotte woke up late the following morning. Hope, who wanted a full-course breakfast his mother always made, awakened her. He walked into her bedroom to see if she was awake. Judging by the look on her face, she was feeling a certain amount of depression, he thought. She took great care of herself and usually looked much younger than her true age.

He asked his mother why she looked so downhearted that morning. Charlotte assured him that everything was fine and that breakfast would be ready shortly. She made pancakes and syrup together with scrambled eggs. Hope could smell the savor of the bacon that sizzled in the kitchen. Additionally, she had freshly squeezed orange juice, sliced strawberries, and blueberries on the side.

That was one of his favorite meals for breakfast. She reached out for the TV remote control and flipped through the channels to select one of their favorite morning shows.

A few minutes after breakfast, she tidied up her living room, as if she wanted to engage in an activity to mask her downhearted feeling. Charlotte then took a long, warm bath. Later, relaxing in the living room, she continued to muse over the movie they had seen the night before.

She compared and contrasted the life of the lead character in that movie to her own life. She recalled both her sad and happy times in her life. She thought about the moments of despair and frustration in her marriage.

Edmund was a supportive and loving husband, she accepted. Nevertheless, he was not perfect. He was sometimes hardheaded, such as when she unsuccessfully tried to convince him to postpone their fishing trip, an aspect of his character that she thought contributed to her current predicament. At one point she went back to her bedroom to keep Hope from seeing her emotionally distraught.

After this intense but subtle mental and emotional outflow, she fell asleep on the couch. Hope never knew his mom to be a day sleeper. He gazed at her as she slept on the couch almost to the point of snoring. He turned off the TV and went to lie down in his bedroom.

At about two p.m., the sound of the doorbell awakened them. Charlotte looked at the wall clock in the living room. She could not believe she had been in bed that late. When she looked through the peephole, she found Beverly in front of the door. Obviously, she grew accustomed to Beverly's unannounced visits to her home. She opened the door for her.

"What are you doing staying so late in bed?" she asked. "It is a beautiful day, today. It should be against the law to stay inside. How is Hope?

"We're both fine. Girl, we got up and had a big breakfast, and since there was nothing else to do, we went back to sleep."

"Your house looks immaculate," Beverly remarked. "Everything is neatly arranged and in order. This house looks so clean."

"Well, you guessed right," she responded. "I hate to be in an untidy house. When Eddie was alive, he helped me with the house chores. Now, I have to do all that by myself."

"Oh, I see. I can now understand why you seemed a little depressed last night. You were thinking about the amount of housekeeping that awaited you. It's hard on a woman to make it on her own."

"Not really," retorted Charlotte. "I am used to hard work anyway. That doesn't mean I did not appreciate Eddie's help when he was alive. On the contrary, I thought the movie was nice. It looked real to me and maybe so to others who may not readily admit it."

"Well said, girl. By the look on your face last night after the movie it appeared to me that, there was something you wanted to say—as if a particular scene drove a particular message home. Trust me, friend. I might be able to help. What are friends for? To share thoughts, help each other. To counsel one another. You were in such a pensive mood that I did not know what to think.

"Come on, spit it out. By the way, you have not even thought about asking me if I wanted something to eat or drink. Your mind must still be out of this world. Let me take it upon myself to do so. I hope you do not mind me looking around the kitchen for some leftovers. I did not cook today, and girl, I'm starving," said Beverly with a smile on her face.

"I don't have anything right now," Charlotte replied. "I threw away the leftovers I kept. That was why I did not make you any offers about food. Aside from that, I did not know you were coming over. I guess I better get in the kitchen and make something fast for us. Breakfast was over a long time ago. Hope might also be hungry by now."

"No girl, you don't have to do that. I will run to one of those fast-food restaurants to pick up something for us. What would you like to have?"

"Oh, cheeseburger, or maybe chicken sandwich, fries, or onion rings. Let's see, I have something to drink at home. What would you like to have, Hope?" she asked.

"I'm not hungry yet. Still full from breakfast. I'll eat later on tonight," Hope replied.

"Well, then. Let me chip in some money to help out," offered Charlotte.

"Oh no. You do not have to do that," stated Beverly. "Let me go and pick up the food. I'll be right back."

Immediately after Beverly left, Charlotte began to cook anyway. She and Hope preferred to have some seafood for supper. She was not keen on fast food. However, she wanted to please Beverly.

When she returned, Beverly was surprised to see Charlotte cooking. Charlotte explained to her the food being prepared was for the next day. The two friends sat down at the dinner table to eat, while Hope watched TV in the den.

Beverly resumed their previous conversation. "You know, girl, I stopped on my way from the restaurant for some gas. I overheard some of the people at the gas station still talking about *Kiddie's Baby*. It must have made a big impact on several people."

"I guess it did," answered Charlotte. "How can one watch such a powerful story, true to life, without being moved? That was one nice movie."

"A fantastic movie. I guess in some ways all of us can identify with it. By the way, we were at the point where you wanted to share your inner feelings about the movie with me," said Beverly jokingly. "That was when I got hungry. Well, now I am full concerning my appetite but hungry for what you wanted to say."

"Girl, this is somewhat hard to say. Let's not talk about it, especially with Hope home with us," said Charlotte, somewhat emotional again.

"Well, friend, if you don't want to talk about it, you don't have to. That is all right with me. I'd rather you get it off your chest than hold it in," responded Beverly with a wry smile.

After a long pause, Charlotte confided in her friend. She openly shared her inner secrets with her. "Let me put it this way. I felt that someone somewhere had written the story of my life. I was born and raised in a small town east of here. As an only child, I knew no other world than that of my immediate family. My parents, who kept a watchful eye over me, usually confined me to the house.

"My dad especially kept a close eye on who came to see me, even my girlfriends. He apparently was suspicious they might be running errands for some guy out there. You know what I mean. He did not openly say it but kept emphasizing that young girls of my age who had many friends usually found themselves entangled in several complications in life. I was afraid to argue with him or respond to his statements. All I did was take in whatever he said and bottle it up.

"My mom had little to say. She was very religious and agreed to most of the things my father said. I had very little social life. In fact, I had little of anything. I could only wear long dresses, skirts, and loose jeans," narrated Charlotte to the attentive and inquisitive Beverly.

"It is good for parents to be protective of their children sometimes," Beverly commented. "However, sometimes some parents are carried away with that without realizing the misery that they might be putting them through. I am of the opinion that your parents were very sincere in their dealings with you, and all that they told you was in your own best interest. I mean, you are pretty, and look at how you turned out."

"Well, in a way I'd agree with you. However, it seemed to me that I was deprived of several social experiences I should have had as a little girl. I saw the girls of my age go out from time to time with friends, and they dressed much better than I did. I mean, they kept up with the latest fashions.

"They went out on dates. Their friends went shopping and did things with them. I had no one of my own with whom to associate. The first and only man I ever knew was Edmund. My aunt introduced him to me.

"She knew him as a young ambitious man from an affluent family. He expressed his desire to get married in his talks with my aunt because he was lonely and perceived most of the women of his age as gold diggers. Given the kind man that he was, at least that was my aunt's perception of him, she felt the two of us would be a perfect match.

"Aunt Laura took pride in making matches, and she was quite successful at it. She also had a lot of influence on my parents. I was very uncomfortable about the whole idea at first because I did not know him, and he was older than I was.

"You know what I'm talking about—that generation gap. However, eventually I developed a great deal of liking and then love for Edmund. I privately agreed to marry him so that I could get out from under my father's umbrella.

"We had a beautiful married life together. He took care of home before anything else. Due to the circumstances that surrounded our courtship, I must admit it took me a while to really, really love him. My love for him was steadily growing at the time he died. His untimely death was an excruciating emotional devastation for me," continued Charlotte with tears flowing.

"I know how painful it can be to lose a loved one," Beverly said. "Someone on whom your entire future rests. It is difficult to understand why things like that happen unexpectedly. However, they do happen. I guess that is why they say life is not fair. Edmund is gone. You will never see him again in the flesh. That is painful but true unless you believe in a divine place called heaven. Then that makes it a little more palatable."

She continued, "I am quite sure that you know there are several things that one could do to ameliorate that unfortunate and painful situation. In fact, you might have put some of them in practice already. I wish I knew a specific suggestion to help you overcome your feelings.

"I have learned over the years that loneliness aggravates a situation like yours. All I can say at this moment, as your trusted friend, is that you should do all you can to rise above it. I am quite sure that you are a strong woman to take care of yourself. I am confident that you will overcome it by and by.

"I do not know whether this idea might help you or not. I was in a similar situation similar to yours. I had two tragic experiences, though not quite as extreme as yours. Besides, I may be wrong, because I may not know or remember all the details of the first one. I mean that put me through horrific nightmares for a long time. In addition, I do not care to remember or share that experience. No, never. I have come to discover that people do not really appreciate what they went through until they hear what others have had to deal with.

"I am beginning to have headaches as I think about the impacts of that nightmare with my first husband. I too married at an early age through parental arrangement to an older businessperson. I never knew exactly what type of business he was engaged in except that I saw people coming in at late hours. They went into a private room and talked. He did a lot of traveling and left me by myself most of the time. He ensured I had everything I needed. We had a chauffeur. He took me anywhere I needed to go.

"However, I was not happy. My first husband, who will remain nameless for now, was a womanizer. I mean he had many women everywhere. Even though I never lacked for money, I was not happy. I tried to get used to that lifestyle, but I could not. You know what I mean. I was jealous that he had other women even though I was the one who lived in his main mansion.

"One day he went to spend the night with one of those women. I asked my chauffeur to take me where he was. He was terrified and refused. Slowly but surely I won him over and assured him nothing bad would happen to him. He then took me to the other woman's house. I asked him to park and wait for me across the street. I went and knocked on the front door of that house. I felt someone looked at me through the peephole. Later, my ex-husband opened the door and asked what I was doing there. I asked him to come back home. He instructed me to take the lead and he would follow soon. I left.

"Next day, he told me we would be going out because he wanted to show me something. I thought he wanted to take me to dinner to make up for the previous night, so I got all dressed up. On the way that evening, I asked where we were going. He said he wanted me to see what happens to people who are disloyal. He took me inside a building. I saw my chauffeur hanging upside down over a pool of blood, dead.

"Later, an organization contacted me to ask for information about him that would lead to his arrest. I was assured my information would be confidential. I would be given a new identity and relocated. I did, and they caught and tried him. He was convicted. I understand he is on death row.

"When we were together, we often talked about having kids of our own. Because of such conversations, I thought he truly wanted children of his own. Having his baby meant a permanent bond with him. However, I thought wrong. As soon as he found out that I was pregnant, he suggested that I have an abortion. The more I resisted, the more he insisted. To cut a long story short, we slept in separate rooms. I went ahead and had his baby anyway after he was convicted. She was a little girl. Under frustration, I placed her with an adoption agency.

"I thought that was the right thing to do. Because of how pretty she looked, I expected some well-to-do couple might adopt and take very good care of her. She had a little birthmark on her left eyelid just like me. A few months later, I longed for my child. However, it was too late to do anything about that. The pain and regret haunted me for a long time. That was the most emotionally painful feeling I ever experienced. I never overcame it. I hope that one day somehow, I shall see her again. That would really make me feel victorious, not a victim of circumstances, you know what I mean?

"I made up my mind to never fall in love again. For a number of years I felt good about my decision. However, it got to a point that I realized I deprived myself of things that I should have under normal and natural circumstances, and so I began to date again.

"After I was relocated here, I met another man. He has turned out to be wonderful. He is a suitable replacement for my first honey. In a way, my relationship with him has helped me overcome the bad experiences I previously had. No pain, no gain. One has to take chances in life. With caution, of course. If you do nothing about an issue, you will get nothing in return, but if you at least try to do something about it, then something will happen. You may win or lose. No one could have convinced me at the time of my distress that sometimes unfortunate events that come our way can lead to greener and greater pastures.

"They may be trials to test our resolve. If we pass the test, then we receive our reward and advance to the next level. There are always different strokes for different folks, as they say. I am expecting him at my house this evening, so I'd better be going. Aside from that, we have to report for work tomorrow morning. If I can help you in any way, my dear friend, feel free to let me know." With that, Beverly got up from her chair and started to show herself out of Charlotte's house.

Charlotte expressed appreciation for the very kind words from Beverly and closed the door. She sat quietly by herself in the living room. Hope was fast asleep. She gave very serious consideration to the points Beverly raised in her discourse. She was very impressed with Beverly's concern for her happiness, as well as her seemingly vast experience in overcoming difficult circumstances that confronted her.

She mentally tried to sort out additional things she might do to rise above her dismal situation due to the loss of her husband. For the rest of that evening, she was intensely preoccupied with that thought—the thought of hope as a will and way to win.

Then suddenly it hit her. She and Edmund had a formula that had guided their dream for Hope to be the chosen one to rescue Avenice and their family's prestige. Certainly, that same formula could be applied to her current problem. The continuity of that thought was interrupted when Hope awakened from his sleep. He was hungry and wanted something to eat before he caught the bus for his campus that evening.

Mending a Broken Heart

Beverly came on time to pick up Charlotte for work. They arrived at work about thirty-five minutes ahead of time. Human Resources turned them over to the vice president of operations to complete additional paperwork. Additionally, his office arranged for someone to get them acquainted with the sewing equipment they would be operating. Naturally, they were nervous on their first day at work.

However, as the day progressed, they became more and more confident with their assignments. Standard operating procedures for that company required them to undergo on-the-job training for a week. After that, they were classified as regular full-time employees.

There were forty-two regular sewing machine operators at that textile plant. Three men were dedicated to supply them with precut bundles of material from the cutting room. Additionally, there were seven designers and three tailors who cut the bundles of material from patterns. A few more employees worked at the warehouse.

There was a small employee cafeteria with an adjoining breakroom. Some of the employees brought their lunch boxes from home. Others purchased their meals at the cafeteria. Charlotte and Beverly worked through their lunch breaks after they got used to their daily routines. They enjoyed their work and had no complaints at all about the working conditions at the plant.

As was usually the case, time flew by because of the fun and focus they devoted to their work. Before long the closing buzzer went off. An entire day's job had been completed successfully. All the employees turned off their sewing machines and left for home.

Charlotte was very tired by the time she got home. Parts of her body ached. Though she enjoyed her new job, she had never worked continuously on a job previously. She did mostly house chores and kept up with her flower gardens. When her husband was alive, he provided for the family. However, things had changed, and she accepted the necessary adjustments she undertook. She rested a while in her living room. Later, she took a nice long shower and went to bed early. She wanted to be well rested for the following day's work.

Both she and Beverly were fast learners. They caught on to the tricks of their new trade quickly. They were elated at the end of the week when they were informed that their training was successful. Finally, they were regular full-time employees. After completion of their training, they were assigned to different sections of the facility. Therefore, they only saw each other during their lunch breaks.

Coincidentally, the men who worked at the cutting room had their lunch breaks at the same time as Charlotte and Beverly. The usual conversations among the employees focused around their activities for each day. However, after a while those conversations gradually became personal.

One of the men who worked in the cutting room made it his business to sit by Charlotte in the lunchroom. His name was Jimmy. He engaged in conversations with her frequently. Charlotte confided her observations of him to Beverly. She thought that fellow had ulterior motives to pursue her if she let her guard down. She gave Beverly the impression that she was not interested in his subtle advances.

Each time Beverly listened with interest to Charlotte's stories regarding that man. Occasionally, she acted indifferently. She wanted Charlotte to make her own decisions about that man. At other times, she encouraged her to just open up and check him out.

Those conversations continued for several days. Jimmy was a persistent fellow. As much as Charlotte resisted his initial advances, she eventually accepted a casual friendship with Jimmy. She swore to Beverly that she would not let the relationship go beyond that. Jimmy was a big person. He stood about six foot four inches tall and probably weighed about 260 pounds.

He was well-manicured and groomed and wore mild scented cologne. He wore glasses, had a short beard, and always smiled as if he had no worries in life. He was also a teetotaler and had many jokes to tell. They often sat together at lunch, and eventually they exchanged phone numbers and called each other occasionally at home.

With the subtle encouraging endorsements by Beverly, Charlotte invited Jimmy to her house for dinner one Saturday afternoon. Hope was home from school that weekend. Charlotte informed Hope they would have a guest for dinner that afternoon.

As she often did, Beverly stopped by Charlotte's house that Saturday morning to provide any assistance in advance of Jimmy's arrival. Jimmy's visit was certainly a big deal. It would be the very first time they would host a man in their home after the passing of Edmund.

By eleven a.m., all the house chores were completed. The bathrooms looked immaculate. The yard was also well manicured. Dinner was cooked by two p.m. All that remained was for Jimmy to show up. Beverly insisted that it would be a good idea for her to stay for dinner. She wanted to be there for her friend, if necessary.

Jimmy pulled in the driveway promptly at four p.m. Charlotte introduced him to Hope. She asked him to make himself comfortable at home. The full-course meal she prepared was simply delicious. It all went well. No red flags showed up. Thus, after dinner, Beverly asked to be excused. She wanted to go to her house and take care of some personal business.

Jimmy stayed over until eight p.m. certainly; he left Charlotte's residence a well-entertained man. Beverly saw him as a nice, responsible man. Charlotte could easily be flattered under normal circumstances. However, at the back of her mind her instincts prompted her to be cautious. The adage, "Not all that glitters is gold" continued to pop into her mind.

Jimmy became a frequent guest at Charlotte's house, especially on weekends. Charlotte told him stories about the way her late husband treated her. Jimmy listened attentively. He imitated the late Edmund's amorous strategies. Occasionally, he took Charlotte to the park, to the movies, or out to eat to free her from having to cook each time he came over. That way they could spend more time together. He also helped her in the kitchen with meal preparation.

Charlotte's conversations with Beverly centered more on her dates with Jimmy and less on the late Edmund. Gradually, it seemed she had found someone to fill the void in her life as a young available woman. Could it be that she could mold Jimmy to stand in her amorous gap for Edmund? she mused.

Someone who would help her overcome her loneliness after the passing of her husband? Only time would tell.

Through it all, Hope kept his impressions and feelings about Jimmy to himself.

The Bitterness of Frustration

Charlotte's relationship with Jimmy progressed steadily. He seemed to be a nice fellow outwardly. Nevertheless, there was a darker side to his real character. As one might say in casual parlance, he was a smooth operator. Thus far, Jimmy's attitude and behavior toward her conveyed an impression that he was a caring, sharing, supportive, and sincere man who held Charlotte's best interest at heart.

He was adept at playing on her emotions to his advantage. So skilled was he in his pretentious manipulations that the innocent Charlotte could not discern the deceptive and cunning games he played on her mind. Briefly stated, Jimmy was a cunning big bad wolf in sheep's clothing. There were several reasons for that.

Though extremely handsome, Jimmy had been an abused and neglected child from a broken home. His dad worked for the railroad company and was away from home most of the time. He was a womanizer. On days he did not work, he entertained himself by drinking alcoholic beverages. While under the influence of alcohol, he abused his wife and son, Jimmy.

Subjection of the innocent and helpless young Jimmy to such appalling, cruel, pathetic, and wicked mistreatment left indelible scars on his psyche. In his early childhood years, Jimmy showed emotional signs of isolation, fear, and distrust of people. He had difficulties with his cognitive skills at school. His teachers wondered why he suffered from low self-esteem, depression, and difficulty in getting along with his classmates. Eventually, he dropped out of school for substance abuse.

Whether by predestination or chance processes, Jimmy one day met an executive director of a charitable organization. That man took an interest in him and his well-being. He placed him in a halfway house and later arranged to have him cleaned up from his substance abuse habit.

Eventually, Jimmy learned a trade at a local vocational school. He went through several unstable romantic relationships. As he grew older, he sobered down significantly, held steady jobs, and had a decent credit history at the time he landed his current job.

Charlotte had an unexpected complete hysterectomy after her husband's death. Several gynecologic laboratory tests done on her showed abnormal transformation of cells in her reproductive system to a cancerous state.

Consequently, she went through menopause. The signs and symptoms of menopause, together with the hard reality that she would no longer be able to conceive another child, were a bitter pill for her to swallow.

Jimmy seemed to care about Charlotte greatly. However, in his heart of hearts he could not accept her son for some unknown reason. Could it be that a blended family was not his idea of a happy family, or did the emotional trauma he suffered as a child occasionally flash back in his mind? He kept that feeling to himself. In fact, he concealed it from Charlotte.

She was unaware of Jimmy's childhood emotional scars. His nonchalant, happy-go-lucky attitude was in fact a cover-up for the deep trauma he had suffered in his childhood. It had evolved into a venomous canker that flashed back in his mind periodically.

He was determined to get Hope out of their way so that he could have Charlotte all to himself. He formulated a systematic and effective scheme to accomplish his objectives by hook or crook.

Jimmy was an observant, fast thinker. However, he was afflicted with a narcissistic personality disorder. Earlier in his relationship with Charlotte, he observed that Hope demanded a lot of his mother's attention, especially when he came home to spend the weekends with her.

His plan was to carefully break those close family ties and then find a way to subject Hope to a series of unbearable emotional pressures. Ultimately, he intended to flush him out of his relationship with Charlotte. He was determined to carry out his devious plan with extreme tact and care so that neither Charlotte nor Hope would discover his intentions prematurely.

He was confident of success for several reasons. Hope lived on campus, which gave Jimmy plenty of time to work on Charlotte's mindset. He found her to be extremely lonely, relatively confused, financially tight, and inexperienced when it came to male-female relationships.

His emotional plan of attack was to provide her companionship, sexual fulfillment, and financial support regularly. He also adopted some of Hope's behavioral characteristics to confuse her. His ultimate intention was to divert all of her attention to himself. Once he accomplished that, then it would be easier to flush Hope out of their relationship.

Consequently, he carefully chose weekend retreats to exotic resorts with Charlotte, and they continued unabated. He showered her with surprise gifts as well. Such pleasant activities kept Hope from coming home on weekends from school. At the same time, they isolated Beverly from Charlotte.

So skillful was he in carrying out his plans that he maintained a firm grip on her even during Hope's presence at home on the long summer vacation.

Charlotte's visits to Hope on campus steadily subsided. His weekly phone calls to her went unanswered. She was away on pleasure trips. Though Hope was not too happy with his mother's new lifestyle, he accepted it and tried to get along with Jimmy. After all, he wanted to see his mother happy, and it appeared she had found that happiness with Jimmy.

Slowly but surely, Charlotte's relationship with Jimmy soared to new heights. He stayed at Charlotte's home for the weekends. He kept the good times rolling.

Around that time, the administrators at Hope's school approved optional online classes for students in their final year. That meant they could complete their final classes virtually from home so that more room would become available for incoming students. During one of their heartfelt discussions in the bedroom, Jimmy convinced Charlotte that it was a good idea for Hope to participate in the online classes.

To his surprise, Charlotte agreed with that suggestion. The idea was that it would provide an opportunity for the entire family to spend more quality time together, and someone would be at home to while they worked. She thought Jimmy was concerned about her and her son's welfare.

Jimmy discussed the plan with Hope as well. Innocently, Hope also fell for the idea of completing his final year virtually. First, he saw it as a challenge he could surmount. Second, he did not care too much about the food on campus. Third, he would have a lot of privacy at home and in his room.

Naturally, Jimmy was quite pleased with the favorable responses he received for his suggestion. Privately, his ulterior motive continued on solid footing. After the implementation of the new changes, Hope noticed a gradual change in his mother's attitude toward him.

She had less and less time to spend with him. She planted in Hope's mind that while quality time with him was good, it was necessary for him to focus more on his online assignments. She seemed less interested in scrutinizing his progress reports as she used to do.

The frequent mother and son communications they once enjoyed gradually ended. Whenever Hope had a problem and needed her opinion, she seemed preoccupied with other things. In fact, she frequently told him directly to act like a mature man, not a little boy! She actually added that he was old enough to make personal decisions and take responsibility for his actions.

Well, maybe he was. After all, Charlotte was his mother. She brought him up that way. Therefore, when she failed to respond to requests for her opinion, he felt ignored or snubbed by her. Things like that went on in the house, sometimes in Jimmy's presence.

Previously, when Hope was dissatisfied with something at home, he expressed his opinion to her. If he felt strongly about something his mother did, Hope reacted by refusing to eat and stayed silent at home the rest of the day. His mother then got his message, and they talked things over. However, he no longer got that soothing reaction from her. Clearly in his mind he suspected something was amiss, but he could not put his finger on it.

Meanwhile Jimmy watched the new developments between Charlotte and her son with a great deal of interest and satisfaction. He had reason to be satisfied. He had not only succeeded in diverting her attention from Hope to him. She had become blind to the impacts of her actions on her son.

Meanwhile, the weekend pleasure trips and surprise gifts continued. Jimmy frequently mentioned his "concern" for Hope's welfare in his daily conversations with Charlotte.

No wonder then that in due time, Jimmy moved in to live with his lover. Charlotte gave Hope the impression that this was a temporary arrangement. After three long months of his continuous presence in their house, Hope was convinced Jimmy did not intend to move out. He was there to stay permanently. He kept a close eye on that situation with a suspicious eye.

Once Jimmy got comfortable he had absolute control over Charlotte's mindset and emotions, he was empowered to initiate an all-out offensive on Hope to flush him out of their relationship. He was convinced he would not face much resistance because he had successfully broken the last vestige of unity between Charlotte and Hope.

Jimmy's relationship with Charlotte took an awkward turn. Flares of intense arguments and temper tantrums, even in the presence of Hope, sporadically marked it. Hope was not used to that kind of family tension. However, later on at night after Hope went to bed, they made up. Jimmy rendered apologies to Charlotte. He reassured her of his unequalled love for her in an intensely affectionate way.

The intensity of the tensions between Jimmy and Charlotte continued sometimes to the point of getting physical. That disturbed Hope a lot, and he spoke to his mother about his disapproval of such events. He reminded her of the peace and tranquility they had enjoyed before Jimmy moved in with them. He suggested she take a fresh look at her current relation with Jimmy. However, she ignored Hope's suggestions.

Charlotte insisted she could take care of herself and that Hope needed to focus on his schoolwork and not meddle with such matters. Those family feuds affected Hope negatively in many ways. Ultimately, he became frustrated but saw no end to those feuds at home.

It was part of Jimmy's plan to create an emotionally unconducive environment for Hope to flush him out of their way. Jimmy was very jealous and possessive of Charlotte. Other than Beverly, Charlotte had no friends. Beverly kept her distance because of Jimmy's behavior. As a result, Hope knew no other person to approach with his family problems. That was a very sensitive and personal matter to discuss with their neighbors.

He was aware of the dream his late dad and Charlotte instilled in him of becoming the family member to restore the economic status of Avenice and regain the family prestige they once enjoyed. Consequently, he expected his mother's support until that goal was met. Evidently, the recent changes at home militated against her doing so.

He could no longer concentrate on his studies and homework. He did not have the peace of mind to do so. His frustrations intensified to the point where he had to seek help from the student health services center. Based on the signs and symptoms Hope relayed to the school physician, he suggested that Hope speak fervently with his mother about the matter. He prescribed a low-dose medication to help him fall asleep.

The sleep tablets helped him get much-needed sleep at night. He sometimes overslept and could not submit his online assignments on time. He also experienced side effects of the medication. Consequently, he was taken off it—which took him right back where he was.

Meanwhile, Hope found a friend in Roger, a young man only a few years older than he was. Hope confided in Roger about his experiences at home. Roger had graduated from the same high school Hope attended. He was unemployed for over a year after his graduation. He was friendly and provided much needed encouragement to Hope.

Roger lived only a few houses down the street from Hope. Therefore, whenever the family feuds flared up between Charlotte and Jimmy, Hope left their house and went to Roger for consolation. The fact that someone gave him an attentive ear helped Hope a lot.

Their friendship grew stronger to the point where Hope considered Roger as an older brother. Roger agreed with the school physician's suggestion that Hope needed to have a very serious talk with his mom. Hope was the man on the spot so to speak, and no one could articulate his feelings to his mom better than he could. Therefore, although he was convinced any conversations with his mom would be ignored, he decided to try anyway.

After three days of serious mental deliberations, Hope summoned enough courage to hold a serious conversation with his mother. Charlotte suggested a Saturday to engage in such a lengthy conversation. She did not work on weekends and could better focus on what he had to say. Hope accepted his mother's suggestion and quietly walked back to his room.

He was disappointed because he did not think he needed an appointment to have a discussion with his mother. Nevertheless, he considered it progress because at least he would have her undivided attention in a few days. It might help if she took time to listen carefully to what he had to say.

For the rest of that week, Hope confined himself mostly to his room. Of course, when Charlotte and Jimmy went to work, he moved about in the house as much as he could. He subscribed to various apps on his cell phone, which had by then become indispensable to him.

He resorted to the use of those apps because Jimmy and Charlotte usually arrived home late from work due to over-time requirements or they stayed close together in the love seat at the family room when they were not feuding.

While waiting for the days to inch along to Saturday, he rehearsed the major points of their pending conversation. He pondered the most effective way to make his mom see eye to eye with him. Slowly but surely, the anticipated time for their meeting drew nearer.

Because sometimes they did not both have to work overtime and the non-working partner had to wait for the other to complete an assigned task at work, Charlotte bought a used car. Jimmy taught her how to drive. She passed her driving test and obtained her driver's license.

On Thursday night that week, Charlotte and Jimmy had a lengthy discussion. Their conversation centered on replacement of a badly damaged door to her car and other items to get it back running again.

They went over the list of estimates Jimmy obtained from three different shops. The cheapest estimate to get the job done was from an auto repair shop a few miles away from where they lived. The insurance coverage on her car would cover the cost of repairs after the deductible plus towing.

Jimmy called in sick the next day in order to take Charlotte's car to the auto repair shop. He wanted to be pres-ent at the shop for the repairs. He considered that necessary because automobile repair shops in the area had a reputation for overcharging customers.

The work was completed, and he brought the car home at about seven that evening. Charlotte was not at home when he arrived. Tired and physically drained from waiting all day on the car, Jimmy relaxed at home with soft music and root beer.

He looked at the clock in the living room. It was about eight p.m. Charlotte had still not made it home. He became concerned. He mused about the cost of payment he made for the deductible in addition to the new set of tires for her car. He checked their mail and looked at his bank statement. It appeared that the check he wrote to pay for the car repairs and tires would barely clear at the bank.

He pondered how hard he worked, even though he missed work on a few occasions. Nevertheless, he had insufficient funds in his bank account within a few days of direct deposit. He became very irritated.

At that point his phone rang. It was Charlotte. She had called to find out if Jimmy made it back home safely. "Where are you?" he asked.

"I'm with Beverly. I will be home shortly," she replied.

"Okay, I'll see you when you get home. Bye," said Jimmy as he abruptly hung up the phone.

He was very suspicious of Charlotte. He did not believe what she said to him on the phone. It had been a while since Beverly visited Charlotte at her home. Therefore, he called Beverly's house phone directly. A man received the call.

"Hello, may I speak to Beverly?" asked Jimmy.

"She isn't home. Would you like to leave a message?" the man at Beverly's house asked.

"Is Charlotte there?" Jimmy asked again.

"Charlotte? This is Beverly's residence. There is no one by that name in this house. You must have the wrong number" was the reply.

"Thank you; bye," responded Jimmy as he hung up.

Jimmy's suspicion of Charlotte grew larger and larger. The truth of the matter was that Beverly's boyfriend had bought a new car that day. Therefore, after work, Charlotte and Beverly drove by to see it. He then took them for a ride around town.

They stopped by a pub to have a drink or two to celebrate the occasion. It was at the time that they returned to his place from the pub that Charlotte called to check on Jimmy. Shortly thereafter, Beverly dropped off Charlotte at her house.

"Hi, honey. When did you make it back?" she asked Jimmy with a smile on her face.

Jimmy did not reply to her question. Charlotte suspected that something must have gone wrong in the house to get Jimmy upset. She went and knocked on Hope's door. After talking to her son, she learned that nothing happened at home. She then suspected that Jimmy was upset because she came home late.

Since she knew how ugly and angrily Jimmy behaved when upset, she quietly went to her bedroom. She took off her work clothes and went to take a bath.

She usually had her second bath of the day around nine p.m. Jimmy was surprised to see her bathing earlier than usual. Thus, he became more suspicious that she had an affair with someone after work and tried to clean up the evidence. After she got through taking a bath, she went back to the living room in her see-through nightgown.

Jimmy ignored her. She warmed up a TV dinner, turned on the TV, and went to sit by Jimmy. "Cheer up, honey. What's the matter with you today?" she asked.

"I don't feel like being bothered, and quit honeying me," he replied.

"Oh, what was the total cost of the work they did? Did they honor their estimate?" she asked.

Jimmy picked up the receipts from under the table and gave them to her.

"Wow, that's a bit more than what they estimated. I guess I would have to reimburse you for part of this bill, when I get my check. I did not realize they would go so far above their own estimate. Let's see, you paid for brand-new tires also. That explains it. Do not worry. You'll get it all back when I get paid." She thought that would clear things up a little and make Jimmy feel better with her reimbursement offer.

Then suddenly Jimmy asked, "Why did you lie to me?"

"Excuse me, lie to you about what?" Charlotte asked, surprised by his question.

"Where were you? Where did you go after work?" asked Jimmy again.

"What do you mean by where did I go? Didn't I call to inform you I was with Beverly?" asked Charlotte.

"But you were not at Beverly's house, goddamn it. Tell me, where did you go?" Jimmy asked again with an angry voice.

"I did not tell you I was at Beverly's house. I said I was with Beverly," responded Charlotte.

"If you were with Beverly, then how come I heard a man's voice in the background? You must think I am stupid," he said.

"Beverly's boyfriend bought a new car, and we stopped by to look at it. He took us for a spin in it. By the time he took us back to his place to get Beverly's car, well, it was getting late, and that was when I called to check on you. Now, what's wrong with that?"

"Liar. Why didn't I hear her voice in the background, if both of you were there?" he said.

"At the time I called, Beverly was using the bathroom," she replied. "Now, why do I have to go through all this? If you don't believe me, call Beverly."

"I don't want to waste my time calling another lying mouth. If she was straight in her dealings, then what was another man doing at her house, anyway?" he asked.

"Well, her cousin is a truck driver for a trucking company at Giboad City. He was in town and stopped by. He always does that."

"How did he get inside the house?" Jimmy asked.

"He called Beverly from where he was, and she told him where she left the house keys."

"It is only a whorish woman who knows the movement of men in town."

"Well, you can believe whatever you want to, but that is the truth," said Charlotte.

"You did not deny what I said; therefore, I know I'm right. I suspect you were with somebody, thinking I might not be home at the time I was. If you were not, why did you take a bath early tonight? Yeah, it was because of fear I might find out the real truth, yeah, that's why," continued Jimmy.

"Let me tell you something, Jimmy. I am getting tired of you accusing me of doing this or that when in fact I am not," she responded in her defense angrily.

"I'm also getting sick and tired of spending my hard-earned money on you and your problems, while you cheat on me. I wonder if anything good can come out of you."

"If that's the way you feel, then why don't you leave?"

"Yeah, I am. I am. One of these days, I will get smart and leave. Then I'd not have to go through all these changes you are putting me through," he replied.

At that point, Charlotte walked away to her bedroom, leaving Jimmy in the living room. He sat all by himself in the love seat. Alone and angry, he reached out for another can of root beer. He turned on the stereo and gazed at the picture of the late Edmund on the wall of the living room. He looked at it more and more closely. He completely focused his attention on it.

For a brief moment, the picture appeared real to him. He felt he was looking at Edmund in the flesh. The late Edmund seemed to blink at him in rapid succession. Suddenly, and unaware of his actions, he got up and moved closer and closer to the picture. The closer he got to it the more real and larger it became to him. Was he in a trance, or was late Edmund really in his presence? he thought to himself! Suddenly, he grabbed the picture, screamed aloud, and flung it to the floor. The resulting noise woke both Charlotte and Hope up.

Charlotte came out of her bedroom to see what had happened. As she tried to pick up the picture, Jimmy pushed her down to the floor with a mean and scary look on his face.

When Hope saw what happened to his late father's picture, he was highly provoked. However, as at other times, he asked himself the same question: *Who should I turn to?*

Back in his room, he battled within his mind to come up with a plausible explanation for his predicament. After several minutes of seemingly fruitless mental deliberations, he fell asleep.

He dreamed about his late father. It was quite a long time since he'd had a dream about him. He recognized him in his dream. He had changed a little from the last time he had a vision about him. The man he thought was his late father in his current dream had a large, sparkling silver coin in his palm. He displayed that coin to Hope and suggested that they play heads or tails. Hope chose tails. Six out of seven flips of the coin turned up heads.

Hope asked if he could have that coin. His father answered in the affirmative by a gentle nod. At that point, Hope reached out for the coin. Suddenly, the noise of thunder and lightning of the early morning rain woke him up.

Hope was very disappointed when he realized it was just a dream. Had his father lived, he thought, life would have been much different for him. Another thought also occurred to him. Why has his late dad changed slightly? Did the process of aging continue after death?

He considered several interpretations of his dream. Baseless and unrealistic as it was, he consoled himself that it was an indication that a large part of his life was destined for success. Only a small part looked gloomy. He did not recall seeing anybody else in the dream. *What could be the significance of that?*

Then he heard slight sounds of movement and whispers. They were those of Charlotte and Jimmy.

CHAPTER

8

Appointment with Death

Charlotte got out of bed late Saturday morning. As she prepared breakfast, Hope went into the kitchen. He reminded her about their scheduled conversation. She asked him to go ahead with what he had to say, as she cooked.

"I'm under terrible pressure, Mom," he said.

"No, no, no. It's too late to change schools again," she responded.

"You don't understand," he said.

"Yes, I do too. I know it can sometimes get very rough when you are about to get out of school. Those teachers pile assignments on you as if you have nothing else to do. I notice you have been staying in your room a lot lately. You have to take it easy sometimes. Give yourself a break. It's good to study hard. But too much studying is not good for your mind."

"I'm not talking about that kind of pressure. I'm talking about what is going on right here. It's unbearable. Oh, Mom, what are the two of you doing to me?"

"What are you talking about? I don't understand."

"I mean what—" Hope hesitated as Jimmy came to the kitchen to check on breakfast.

"Hey … hey! What's going on around here?" he said.

"I know breakfast is late," Charlotte said. "I will be done in a minute. Hope, why don't you wipe off the breakfast table?" .

Jimmy's untimely presence in the kitchen interrupted their long-awaited conversation. All along, Hope foresaw this conversation with his mother as private and confidential. Under these circumstances, he saw no chance of continuing with their talk in privacy.

So he left the house to visit his friend Roger, who he knew would take time to hear him out and give him words of encouragement. On that day, Roger was invited to a birthday party in Caprice, a town almost thirty miles away from Avenice.

Roger had a great sense of humor. He listened attentively to the latest developments at Hope's house. He opted to invite Hope to accompany him to the party. Roger thought a change in environment might be good for him.

At first, Hope was reluctant to accept his invitation. He recalled what happened when he previously attended another party with his two dorm neighbors on campus. Roger assured him that nothing like that would happen. To add to the excitement at that party two surprising events were supposed to happen. First, Roger would perform a few magic tricks. Second, two identical twin sisters, Caroline and Rosaline, who attended the same school as Hope, were going to find out who their blind dates were at the party. That made Hope feel better.

For example, two identical neighborhood twins, Charlie and Victor, who attended the same school as Hope, and two twin sisters, Rosaline and Caroline, were going to be on blind dates at the party. That made Hope feel better. He accepted Roger's invitation. Roger's elder brother had agreed to let him borrow his car for that evening. The invitation to the party soothed Hope's frustrations somewhat for the time being.

The party was crowded. Several teenagers from nearby towns were also present. The disc jockey was quite good. He played the latest popular songs that had almost everyone up on their feet at the dance floor. There was hardly a place available to sit down because of the great crowd of people. Roger was a little uneasy because he thought his other invited guests, Rosaline and Caroline, had not yet showed up at the party.

Suddenly, as the disc jockey played a very slow number, Roger saw Rosaline dancing with some person under the dim lights. He felt a sigh of relief. However, Roger wondered who the person was who was dancing with her. No wonder then that immediately after that song; Roger quickly went to meet his friends, Caroline and Rosaline, who sat at the corner of the dance hall.

"What's happening, Roger? Sorry we came so late," said Caroline.

"Well, I know young ladies take their time to get all dressed up for occasions like this. I hope, my darling friends, that you'll take your sweet time to hear me out on what I'm about to say."

"What is it, partner?" retorted Rosaline. "You always seem to have something new to say or do. It is never a dull moment with you."

"Actually, it is a big surprise I have for the two of you pretty ladies. I hope you have room enough in your nests to take what I'm about to dish out to you," he replied.

"Well, break it down friend," said Caroline, clearly curious. "We are all ears. We feel like getting into some excitement tonight." Rosaline was a quiet onlooker at this point.

Roger held a piece of folded paper in each hand, with the names *Charlie* and *Victor* written on them. He stretched out his hands and asked Caroline, "Hey, sweet Caroline, make a choice. What you pick is what you get, girl. Good luck."

The folded paper she picked was the one that read, *Charlie*. Thus, Rosaline got the other marked *Victor* as her surprise date.

"Come with me and meet my friends," said Roger to the twin sisters, who stared at each other in the face. They were pleasantly surprised. They apparently liked what they saw. In addition, what they saw was what they got.

The nervous identical twin brothers knew neither where to begin nor what to say to their blind dates. So Roger broke the ice and did most of the opening conversation. His match-making skills worked out well. The DJ played a variety of soft music. The couples took to the floor and danced so close to each other that one might think they had known each other for quite a long time.

Roger was gratified. He had achieved what he wanted to do. He displayed his magical skills to the heavy applause of everyone. The mood at that party was enlivening. They seemed to have a great time.

Caroline and Rosaline always had their way with their grandmother with whom they lived. She was partially blind. They went out and came home as they pleased. They paid little or no heed to what the old woman told them. To them experience was the best teacher.

The party was so pleasant that everyone expected it to last until daybreak. However, neither Roger nor his companions intended to stay that late. At about 10:45, Roger signaled them that it was time to leave.

From all indications, everyone had a great time at the party. Charlie and Victor filled Roger in on their interactions with their blind dates. They hit it off so well that they planned a follow-up visit the following weekend.

Roger's elder brother had purchased a brand-new tire a week or so before the party. He intended to replace one of the front tires, which had a bald area, with the new tire. However, he never got around to changing that defective tire. He kept procrastinating each time it dawned on him to take care of it.

On their return trip home from the party, as they descended a steep hill, they had a blowout in one of the front tires of the car. Roger somehow lost control of the car. Within a few flashing seconds, as they travelled at high speed, the car ran off the road and plunged into the adjacent valley. Miraculously, Hope was thrown out of the car, which tumbled over into the valley and continued to roll downhill.

A state trooper picked them up on his radar a few moments earlier. He turned at the next intersection to ticket them for speeding. However, he quickly saw what had happened, stopped, and went to their rescue. Hope was not badly hurt, though he was very shaken up. Unfortunately, his other companions in the car were pronounced dead at the scene. They were only a few miles away from Avenice. Death had laid its cold, icy hands on them only a few short miles away from Avenice.

Hope did not know how to take the pronouncements on his friend and companions. Only a few minutes earlier they had been reflecting on the pleasant moments they experienced at the party. Suddenly, they were gone. Gone forever.

In a twinkling of an eye, they passed away into the realms of the dark world of the dead. A place where no one could return to warn you about the afterlife. He was immensely hurt and confused. He could not believe it.

The loss of his close friend and confidant, Roger, further aggravated his frustration. He was very lonely. Yet he summoned an inner strength to complete all his online assignments to meet requirements for his high school diploma. That was quite an accomplishment.

The fanfare and big celebration he hoped for at that event never materialized. He wondered whether the desire and expectation of being the avenue by which Avenice would rebound from its economic decadence and his family would regain their prestige might never be fulfilled.

As a mother, Charlotte could tell that her son was completely withdrawn from her. She tried to show a certain amount of concern for him, especially as Hope stayed in his room almost all the time when she was home. However, it was too late. Sustained loneliness and frustration had inflicted much damage on his psyche.

Her concern did not last that long anyway, especially when Jimmy explained to her that sometimes young men went through certain changes due to circumstances beyond their control and that Hope probably needed some time alone to get himself together.

Fortunately or unfortunately, a youth center opened in Avenice. The huge promotions of that facility persuaded Hope to register there. He identified with the vision and mission of the center.

The youth center organized weekend car wash events to raise spending money for its membership. Additionally, the center offered free music lessons. Hope thought it would be fun to learn how to play the guitar. His real reason was to engage in some activity to relieve his frustration as well as earn a little pocket money for himself.

There were not that many jobs in Avenice, and he thought if he became proficient at playing the guitar, he could get together with the new friends he would make at the center to form a pop group that could catapult him to stardom and out of his misery.

Hope followed up on his convictions. He duly registered at the youth center. The center offered what they said they would. Within a few days, Hope adjusted to his new environment, and he felt better than he had only a few days before. He also picked up quickly on the guitar lessons. His earnings from the weekend car washes provided enough cash to buy a used guitar of his own.

There were quite a few nice people at the center. However, after the unexpected death of his friend and confidant, Roger, Hope did not wish to get close to anyone. Still, the supervisors at the center found Hope to be a likable sort. Furthermore, they observed that he was a serious-minded young man. He maintained a keen focus on his assignments, both indoors as well as outdoors. He required minimal supervision. Hope had a neat appearance. They assigned him to clean the cafeteria on weekends, when the regular cleanup crew did not work. That was great news for Hope. He would not only be able to afford the guitar, but also additionally wean himself off his mother financially. He even imagined saving enough from his earnings for other necessities. So successful and progressive was Hope at the youth center that slowly his frustrations subsided.

Even Jimmy noticed that Hope was gradually regaining his self-confidence. The youth center trusted him enough to give him the keys to the building. Thus, anytime he was unhappy at home, he went there and played the guitar to ease his mind. However, that was not for long. Soon, Jimmy went back to work again with his devious but subtle schemes. He turned up the heat a notch on Hope. He complained about everything Hope did at home. But he did it with a smile on his face to convey the impression that all he was trying to do was correct Hope's "mistakes" so that he could learn from them.

Privately, Jimmy fabricated some of his accusations against Hope. He tried to get Hope to believe that he could not do anything right without his guidance. Jimmy would sometimes place his hands on Hope's shoulders, look him in the eye, and say something like "My man, Hope. Everyone tells me you are a good young man. But I wonder what you're good for!" For a while, Hope surmounted Jimmy's mental and emotional pressures.

One Saturday morning Jimmy falsely accused Hope of doing something wrong in the house. Charlotte was not home at that time but was working overtime. When she returned home and was told what Hope allegedly did, Hope maintained his innocence. Jimmy expected her to reprimand her son anyway, and when she didn't do so, that sparked a major feud in the house, such as Hope had rarely witnessed.

As usual, Hope left for the center. His associates observed he was not himself that day. They did not insist on knowing the reason for his unusual attitude. He played a few games of ping-pong and a volleyball game, and finally he picked up the guitar to play a few chords, after which he felt better. At the end of the day, and after everyone left, Hope cleaned the cafeteria, as usual.

Alone again, he reflected on what had taken place at home. He became nervous and took a coffee break. However, the coffee dispenser did not work. Therefore, he entered the office of the kitchen supervisor, where he found a hot plate. After he made the coffee, Hope went to the adjoining cafeteria. He continued with his work and intended to return for an additional cup.

He did not turn off the hot plate. He pondered his plight as he drank his coffee. The more he thought about how dismal and gloomy his whole life had become, the more additional hurtful things arose in his mind.

At the point where he felt extremely bad he rounded up his work and went to the music room to play the guitar as he previously did to get calm. Frustration can lead to confusion and forgetfulness. No wonder then that after he played the guitar for a while, he left for home and forgot to go back and turn off the hot plate in the kitchen supervisor's office. At home, he took a shower and went straight to bed. The center did not operate the following day. Thus, he slept and intended to get up late the following morning.

Around midnight, sounds of sirens from ambulances, fire engines, and police cars awakened most of the people in the neighborhood. While Hope slept soundly, the youth center was on fire. The resulting conflagration inflicted serious damage to the facility before it was completely subdued by the firefighters.

A thorough investigation determined that someone had left a hot plate on in the kitchen supervisor's office. The office windows were not completely closed that night. Consequently, it was possible that the strong winds that preceded an oncoming storm blew several sheets of paper from the supervisor's desk. The sheets of paper probably ended up on the hot plate and started the fire. The investigators wanted to know who had left the hot plate on.

The following morning, Hope learned about the fire at the youth center and its possible cause. He recalled he had made a cup of coffee Saturday night by boiling water on that hot plate. Hope told the truth when asked by his superiors at the center and admitted that he made coffee Saturday night while he worked because the coffee machine was out of order, and he must have left it on.

His supervisors admired his honesty and integrity. However, the damage caused by the fire was too high to be ignored. Thus, they fired Hope from his job. That was a major blow to Hope. He thought life was not fair. However, that was the way it was.

That incident gave Jimmy something to hammer on. He continued to insinuate that Hope was a good-for-nothing young man. How else could he explain himself to anyone? Better yet, could he and Charlotte trust him to keep their house safe while they were away at work or on weekend trips? Everything he did went wrong. Very wrong. No matter what he said, no one believed him. How much more could he take and survive?

He saw no hope of an end to his frustration. He could not turn to Angie or her parents because they had moved away. His close friend and confidant, Roger, had died tragically and suddenly. Medical science did not help him much, and now the last vestige for Hope to turn his life around at the youth center had proved futile. Again, he asked himself, *Who should I turn to?*

He was convinced there was not much left for him to do or accomplish in Avenice. He remembered the dream he'd had of a man who looked like his late father. Hope reasoned that if there were any years of success in his life, as he interpreted that previous vivid dream, and of overcoming his problems, they awaited him elsewhere. So he seriously considered leaving home.

CHAPTER 9

To a Destination Unknown

On a Saturday morning, Hope got up very early from bed. He took stock of all that had happened in his life. After very careful and pensive deliberations, he was convinced that the best thing for him to do was to leave home.

He did not see an end in sight for the senseless life-wrecking experiences he was going through at home. He carefully reflected on his parents' desire for him to be the channel through whom the economic well-being of Avenice, as well as their family's prestige, could be restored. Those aspirations had become part of his ultimate goal.

He emotionally and mentally bought into that vision at an early age and was committed to making that happen somehow, one day soon. After the death of his father, suddenly, his entire life seemed to have turned upside down. However, time was on his side!

Nothing he did seemed to work in his favor except that he had completed his high school education under trying circumstances. The mother he so dearly loved and looked up to as a strong tower of hope was head over heels in love with a manipulative, malicious, and heartless stranger.

She could not see the devastation and havoc he had brought on their hitherto serene, ambitious, and motivated family—a determined family resolved and unwavering in their persistence to regain the economic growth of Avenice, as well as their family prestige.

Hope wondered why fools fell in love. He recalled part of the lyrics of one of the songs played at the party he attended with Roger, that "loving eyes don't ever see."

Minutes after Hope finally made up his mind to leave home, he heard his mother doing some work in the kitchen. Regardless of the circumstances that caused him to take such a drastic decision, he thought it was a good idea, as a matter of common courtesy, to let her know about his decision. Whether she made time to listen to him or not would not matter. He went into the kitchen and found her washing dishes left in the sink the night before.

"Good morning, Mom."

"Good morning. Why are you up so early?" she asked.

"I think this is a convenient time for me to complete what I started to tell you the other day," Hope responded.

"Oh, yes, we were interrupted by Jimmy. You may continue where we left off."

"You may not like what I have to say but I'm sure it would not matter to you, anyway. As I told you the other day, I have been under pressure, more pressure than I can bear. The pressure was not from schoolwork, as you thought. It was from right here at home. I have noticed a great deal of change in you, and in this house. You are no longer the loving and caring mother I once knew. Neither is this house the pleasant, peaceful, happy home we once enjoyed. I am sure you know what I'm talking about."

"No, I don't. What do you mean?" she asked.

"I'm talking about the neglect, the quarrels, arguments, the fights. You are putting me through too many changes. Apparently, you cannot see it. Mama, what have you become? Can't you see what is happening to us?"

"You are too young to understand these things. Who have you been talking to, anyway?"

"You have always told me I was old enough to make up my mind and take responsibility for the decisions I make whenever I had a problem and needed your guidance. Now you are telling me that I am too young to understand these things. Where were you when I needed your help? You have neglected me lately. You have showed me no parental love or care like you used to.

"I understand very well that I am no longer a baby," he continued, "but wasn't that the way you raised me? Who else could I have turned to but you? I have nobody else. Now, ever since Jimmy moved in with us, there has never been any peace of mind in this house, at least for me. I felt tormented because of the feuds, the family tensions and all. I never saw Dad lay his hands on you or push and shove you around. I am unhappy. I am severely frustrated.

"Remember the incident at the youth center? I could no longer concentrate. You were convinced the youth center burned down because of my carelessness. Jimmy keeps insisting that I am good for nothing. That was not so. Do you have any idea what the deep frustrations I went through in this house did to me? I was upset. So upset I forgot to turn off the hot plate in the kitchen supervisor's office. I cannot go on like that. I cannot foresee any changes for the better in this house. I mean, how much more can I take?

"I have done a lot. An awful lot to survive these pressures without losing my mind. You told me I was old enough to take care of myself. I developed mental toughness up to a point. See this rubber band? You can only stretch it up to a point; beyond that, it will break. So now, I have made a decision. In order to save myself and realize my destiny, the destiny you and Dad had for me, in order to let everyone have his or her space and be at peace, at least the way I see it, I must leave this house very soon.

"I will go wherever I can find happiness. I will go wherever I can find a way to fulfill my destiny. I know I have the <u>will</u> to do so. I will persevere in my <u>will</u> and find a way to realize my destiny. Nothing will hold me back. Absolutely nothing! Where exactly must I go? I do not know. However, I have faith it will all work out for my good. All I know right now is that I must live up to my name, *Hope*. That's all I have right now," he concluded.

"Why are you talking like that? Who is putting these things in your head lately?" Charlotte asked.

"After going through all the changes I've been through I should know whether I'm wanted around here or not. You do not have to worry about me anymore. I can clearly see you are doing quite well, and in good hands."

"Watch your mouth," she retorted. "I hope you know what you are talking about."

"Thank you for hearing me out. At least I got it off my chest," said Hope as he walked back into his room with tears streaming down his cheeks.

Charlotte was speechless for a moment. She sighed, and then continued with what she did before Hope came to talk to her. She couldn't bring herself to take him seriously.

Later that morning, Jimmy had an invitation to a party at a nearby town. Because of the recent tensions in the house, he was unsure whether Charlotte would accompany him to the party. He told her about it anyway. To his surprise, she took him up on his invitation.

As Hope lay quietly on his bed, he overheard their conversation. They intended to leave early in the afternoon to beat traffic. Alone again at home, Hope formulated his trip to an unknown destination. He packed a few clothes and other items in a haversack. He slipped into a pensive mood as he sat on his bed. He continued to figure out the best way to leave.

He next went to the kitchen and warmed up the leftover food his mother had prepared the night before. He loaded up his plate with a substantial amount of food, and left a note on the dining table, which read, "The Last Supper." He took a short nap after that meal. He needed to rest well for his intended journey to an unknown destination.

He woke up at about two o'clock the next morning. That was more than a nap. It was a very relaxing sleep. He needed that because it had been a while since he had enjoyed such a refreshing and peaceful sleep. He went to use the bathroom.

When he came out of the bathroom, he realized he was still all alone in the house. The master bedroom light was on. Neither Charlotte nor Jimmy slept with the lights on. He walked to the living room to be sure he was all alone in the house. They had not returned from the party from the previous evening. Hope looked through the window. He did not see his mother's car parked in the driveway, as usual.

He went back to his room. Posted on his wall was a calendar. It had the picture of a train that navigated through meandering railroad tracks in a vibrant mountainous terrain. The idea then occurred to him to leave on the early morning train. In less than three hours, it would pass only a short distance away from their house through Avenice. Due to ongoing maintenance work on the tracks, the trains were compelled to negotiate that portion of the tracks near their house at snail speed.

Meanwhile, all was not well with Charlotte and Jimmy.

On their way back from the party they were stopped at a checkpoint set up by the police looking for a stolen car suspected of being used to transport illegal drugs and other contraband. One of the police officers became suspicious of Jimmy in the driver's seat. He was nervous. Jimmy had remained a teetotaler for several years. However, during recent events he had become a social drinker.

The police officer noticed that the serial number on the documents Jimmy had on Charlotte's car did not match that affixed on the driver's door. That made him the more suspicious, and he asked Jimmy to step out of the car. Smelling alcohol on Jimmy's breath, the officer subjected him a breathalyzer test.

Jimmy explained to the police officer that he had the car door replaced a few days earlier with one obtained from a junkyard. That accounted for the discrepancy in serial numbers. However, he did not have his receipt in the glove compartment.

The police officer did not believe him. He detained Jimmy, pending further investigation of his claim. In talking to Charlotte, the police officer further discovered that she too had been drinking and did not have any identification on her.

By the time Hope got through taking his bath, and ensured that all he wanted to leave behind was in order, it was time to leave. He walked through the living room on his way out.

He caught sight of the damaged picture of his father, which Jimmy in an angry rage had smashed on the floor. He picked it up and then paused for a moment as he looked closely at it. He took the picture out of the frame, put it in his haversack, and walked out the door.

The rail track was within walking distance from their house. A few minutes later, he saw an old cargo train, which was ideal for his purpose. It slowly approached him at his vantage point. He felt the vibrations of the heavy train, as it virtually inched its way toward him.

The train driver sounded the alarm to alert everyone of the passage of a moving train. Hope watched the engine go by him. It was a very long train. Three engines pulled the seventy-seven cars, loaded flatbeds, and huge tanks it transported.

He knew this was his chance to get out of town. If he missed this train, it might be a while before another one came along. Therefore, he must get aboard. At last, he ran quickly, precisely caught hold of the ladder at the back of the last caboose, and got on the train. He had a long ride ahead of him.

The train slowly passed through the outskirts of Avenice. From his vantage point at the back of the caboose, he saw the fading lights of Avenice. The train made turns at various points as it by passed the western fringes of Avenice.

It travelled through several small towns until eventually at dusk it arrived at its final destination for that day. Giboad City was a large terminal hub for land, sea, and air traffic. It had a population of about five million inhabitants. It had a diversified economy that made it stable.

Hope got off the train and quietly snuck into the train terminal. His haversack hung over his left shoulder. He had no particular place to go in the city. He looked to his right and found a vacant seat. He sat there and pondered how he would survive in this strange city.

He looked through the windows of the station and was amazed to find numerous cars and trucks running at snail pace on the congested highways. Never in his entire life had he seen such an ocean of people crammed at a single location.

The frequent sounds of sirens from ambulances and police cars made him nervous. He was afraid to leave the confines of the train terminal. He estimated that the number of people he saw around the train terminal alone could out-number the largest gathering of people who turned out for the biggest events in Avenice.

He had doubts whether he would fit in here. However, he was determined to try, no matter what it took. Returning to Avenice was not an option. He was tired and worn out from the long uncomfortable train ride from Avenice. A short nap in his seat might get him refreshed enough before he ventured into the city.

He was also hungry. Left with the choice of staying where he thought it was relatively safe or venturing out into the town to satisfy his hunger were both unpleasant options. Nevertheless, he had to do something fast before nightfall.

Hope made up his mind to take his chances with venturing into town. He had no cell phone on him.

He picked up his haversack, combed his hair, and boldly walked out of the station. He felt funny because he observed that almost everyone he passed by along the way turned and looked at him.

He could not think of a reason why he was the center of attraction in town. He entered a fast-food stand located a mile or so away from the station. There he overheard some-one remark to another person to turn around and look at that country boy.

After that remark, Hope made observations and com-parisons between himself and those around him. He wanted to figure out how they knew he was from the country. He noticed a difference in hairstyle.

Most of all, he did not see anyone else who wore the same type of boots he wore. That, he thought, distinguished him from the rest and accounted for why they looked at him strangely. He ate as fast as he could and went back to the train station.

He picked up a newspaper someone had left behind and began to read it. Before long, he dozed off in his seat. When he woke up, he looked through the pages of the newspaper he had. As if by chance or predestination, he came across the address of a humanitarian organization in town.

He paced back and forth around the inside of the station. He stumbled on one of the uniformed station employees who got off work. He approached him and asked, "Sir, are you done for the day?"

"Yes, I'm on my way home. It's been a long day," he replied as he walked out of the building.

"Well, sir. Which way are you going?" Hope asked.

"To the east of town."

"Is that somewhere near this address?" Hope showed the address to the man.

"Let's see. Not really. That means going about two miles off course. Why, you need a ride?"

"Yes, I do," responded Hope instantly.

"Come on. You have got yourself a ride. That would give me the opportunity to stop by and check on an old relative who lives near there," the man said.

They continued their conversation in the stranger's car. "I saw you sitting at the station all day," the man said. "I wondered if you'd ever leave."

"I did not see you," responded Hope.

"Oh, I'm one of the security guys at the terminal. I watch the movements of people on the security monitor," he said.

"That's neat. I did not know I would ever leave my seat. I expected someone to pick me up, but he never showed up," replied Hope. For some reason, Hope was hesitant to reveal the truth about himself. He realized he was either cautious or scared.

"That's one of the things I hate, you know," the man said, shaking his head. "I get mad when someone keeps me waiting for hours on end, and never shows up."

"I know what you mean. It is a terrible feeling."

"Yes, it's terrible. However, people do it all the time around here. I have seen people stranded at that station many a time, with nowhere to go. Some end up staying at cheap motels, while others sleep at the station. I don't know, man. It is becoming such a big problem here. There are quite a few places in town supported by certain charitable organizations. They provide temporary housing for needy people until they can get on their feet.

"There's quite a few people here with good hearts," he continued. "You may be lucky if you run into one of those. Some have done wonderful things for strangers. I read some time ago about people who did great things for strangers, not knowing they actually entertained angels."

"You mean they can stay there for free?" asked Hope.

"Yes, for a short time only. Now, let me see that address again. I believe we're close to your destination," he said.

Hope showed him the address.

"Now, wait a minute. That is the building right there. Yeah, that looks like one of the places I mentioned. That is it. I did not realize that was the place you were looking for. You only showed me the address. It would have been easier for me if you gave me the name of the place. I hope you can get in tonight. They might appreciate you at least saved their shuttle van driver a trip to the train station, huh?"

"There you go! It will all work out, I believe. Thanks a lot for the ride. I appreciate it," Hope replied as he got out of the car.

A sign posted at the doorway eventually led him to the office of the supervisor on duty. Hope presented his plight to the supervisor, who was sympathetic to Hope's plight. He had one spot left for Hope to stay for a few days.

Residents at that facility were required to return to their dormitories by eight p.m. each night. The organization financially supporting them had made that rule. It was past dinnertime. Therefore, nothing was available for Hope to eat. He was, however, very satisfied because he had a place to stay. He put his things in place, took a shower, and went to bed.

C H A P T E R

10

Survival in Giboad City

Hope woke up at about six a.m. the next morning. He rejoiced over the amazing and surprising successes he had experienced yesterday. He preoccupied himself with thoughts about survival in his new environment.

There was always some concern about the unknown, especially in a large metropolis where he had no social connections. Other than, a strong faith he nurtured about his ultimate destiny, a still small voice within, gave him the idea that nature itself might hold another plan for his life. His challenge then was to somehow identify and merge the two plans together. Hope used the serene time he had on hand at his temporary abode to delve deep into his heart, mind, and soul. He imagined and visualized his destiny in ways he never had previously. It was like a spiritual awakening that took place deep within him.

His parents, especially the late Edmund, articulated their desire for him to be the deliverer to one day salvage the decadent economic plight of Avenice and regain their family prestige. Hope was a spiritually sensitive young man. He had a premonition that his ultimate destiny was already formulated in the spiritual realm. He continued to believe that in due time a physical manifestation would come to pass openly. Whether that happened by fate, chance processes, destiny, or purpose remained to be seen. No matter what, Hope had a strong will to keep moving forward.

He wondered how he could unearth the capabilities embedded in him to fulfil that role. That did not make sense to the carnal mind. Outwardly, circumstances beyond his control had made him an impoverished young man in need of financial intervention. Yet, in his dismal financial state, something deep within assured him that he had the spiritual power within him to accomplish great things he never imagined.

He had been through enough harsh and painful experiences to know that his only hope for success in that regard was outside himself. He was at the point where circumstances had directed him to appeal to charity, in hopes that somewhere on the horizon a breakthrough might come his way.

During the very trying times in his last year of high school, in particular, he took consolation in watching sermons preached by renowned televangelists. In one particular teaching, he heard the preacher emphasize the promise of God and the exhortation of mercy to those who perceived themselves as failures in life, those who were down at heel, broken, and crushed by the uncertainties of life.

His previous experiences in Avenice had taught him that the point where the strength and wisdom of humans failed marked the beginning of the matchless and undisputable power of the God of creation in the affairs of His chosen. The almighty could be depended upon to select and appropriately crack open the door of hope.

His faith assured him that God would subsequently pour out a blessing on those who learned to wait on Him without a doubtful heart or wavering faith in His lovingkindness, tender mercies, and righteous judgment. *However, why would He do that?* he mused. Because they are those who need His mercy the most.

Second, God does not look at our physical appearance and excellences. Rather, He looks at our hearts, knows our needs, and satisfies our emptiness in accordance with His will. A brokenhearted person who is poor in spirit would most likely be the one who best testifies to divine grace and listens to the word of God to build his or her faith.

Hope used those trying times in Avenice to read voraciously. He read somewhere that God owned the universe and all that was in it. Consequently, the God of the universe was able to give freely and willingly to those who asked of Him. It is such a person to whose ears the tidings of a salvation by grace through faith would sound harmonious rather than like empty words of cacophony. Hope had not quite understood such teachings at the time he heard or read them. Now, he did.

The question he asked himself was how could he find a way to merge the desires of his heart together with those of nature on grounds of the faith in that unique and unsearchable God of the universe who had guided him thus far? If he could, then he might well be on his way to the success in accomplishment he sought. He expressed thanks and appreciation while in that pensive state of mind for the little molehills he had already surmounted.

Everything seemed to have fallen in place for his good thus far. His gut feelings told him he would make it. By sheer determination and boldness, he had left Avenice. He left Avenice with practically nothing except the clothes in his haversack. He embarked on his new life with virtually nothing. So far, he had kept his head above water.

As such, Hope continued to look at the bright side of life. The visions he had in Avenice played repeatedly in his mind. He was determined to follow his instincts, boldness, determination and persistence to make it in Giboad City. His present priority was to locate a job, find an abode of his own, and be as independent as possible of anyone. If he could accomplish that, then he reasoned his objectives would continue to take shape.

Most of the fellows who lived at the mission house learned about the new addition to their group late that morning. Some of those who were curious or inquisitive stopped by Hope's room to chat with him and welcome him. As was expected, they were mostly interested in finding out how and why Hope got there, and how long he had to stay.

In his conversations with them, Hope discovered they all had problems of various sorts, but he did not reveal his own to them. He learned a lot about the city from those of them who were natives of that city. Some of the stories he heard were encouraging, while others were quite frightening and discouraging.

However, he did not allow the experiences of others to affect him negatively. Alone once again in his room, Hope continued with his strategy of survival in Giboad City.

He jotted down on a small notepad his projected cost of transportation to scout the city in search of a job or to go back and forth to work if he found a job. He also wrote down what it might cost for an efficiency apartment and associated utilities. He had no insurance coverage and was aware of being careful as he went about in the city. At least he knew his room and board were taken care of for about ten days.

Once that allotted time was up, he would not be readmitted in the future so that others might have their chance for such free housing assistance as well. He was unskilled and had no previous stable job experience aside from his part-time job at the youth center in Avenice.

Finally, he decided that he had done enough planning for the time being. What he needed to do was to relax the rest of the day and start looking for work the next day. He was specifically interested in a busboy position or kitchen help so that after he left the mission house he could continue to have decent meals, either free or at a discounted price. His job, he thought, must be within reasonable distance from where he stayed to minimize transportation cost as well as travel time.

The supervisor on duty the next morning was gracious enough to offer Hope some money to ride the public bus as he desperately looked for a job. He additionally provided him a copy of the bus schedule. Since he did not have a cell phone, he went over the bus route with the supervisor to ensure he could find his way back to the mission house without getting lost.

The bus service at Giboad City was very efficient. Hope got on the next bus, and within minutes, he saw a string of restaurants on either side of the main road into the downtown area. He got off the bus and put in applications at almost all the restaurants he saw until, near exhaustion, he returned to the mission house.

His job search continued for the following two days without success. On the third day, however, as Hope got ready to go job-hunting again, he heard a knock on his door. It was the day supervisor. He informed him he had a call downstairs. The call was from one of the restaurants where he had put in an application for employment.

They had a dishwasher position open. If he was interested, he needed to report for an interview for that position at ten a.m. that day. He was pleasantly surprised and shed tears of joy. He proceeded to catch the bus to that restaurant.

He arrived in plenty of time to fill out the necessary paperwork to complete the hiring process after his brief interview. His supervisor introduced Hope to the kitchen staff.

A seasoned dishwashing employee gave Hope on-the-job training. Because he was a fast learner, he caught on to his new job and was soon ready to be on his own.

When work was over, he caught the bus back to the mission house. This was his first regular job. He had never stood continuously for several hours doing a particular job. He hoped his body would get used to taking that much strain after a while.

Hope worked the rest of that week. His approved time to stay at the mission house would be up the following Sunday. He expressed gratitude and appreciation for the help he had received from that mission house.

Hope packed his personal belongings neatly. He signed his release papers and relocated to a YMCA facility that was within walking distance from where he worked.

There was a large carnival and convention in town that week. Consequently, the local restaurants were flooded with customers. On such busy days, Hope was asked to work with the more experienced dishwasher in the kitchen. Additionally, he helped the busboys. He did his best to keep up with his job.

He of course was nervous each time he bused the tables. On one occasion as he bused a particular table, Hope bumped into a woman who was sitting down after she made a trip to the salad bar. He knocked her of balance. She dropped her bowl of salad on a woman seated next to her.

Her escort was furious and would not accept Hope's apology. He demanded to speak with the headwaiter. The woman on who the salad was wasted was the wife of a prominent personality in town. He and his wife were regular customers of that restaurant. Naturally, she was elegantly dressed.

Unable to handle the unintended embarrassment, she and her husband got up and left the restaurant. Unfortunately for Hope, that day the manager of the restaurant made courtesy rounds in the restaurant to ensure everything operated smoothly, and their customers were satisfied. He heard about that unfortunate incident and immediately asked the kitchen supervisor who hired Hope about his previous restaurant experience.

After learning he had none, he became furious. He demanded Hope's immediate termination. He could not afford to lose valued customers at the expense of an inexperienced employee. They paid Hope for the time he worked. His paycheck would be ready the following Friday.

Surprised and shocked at how fast he had lost his job, he proceeded to the YMCA. He learned that due to a glitch in their computer system, his room was reassigned to someone else. They directed him to a nearby facility where he could rent a room by the day.

He secured a place there and started job-hunting again. By that time, life's experiences had taught him that if one window of opportunity closes, another one opens elsewhere. That night he engaged in a conversation with one of the young men who stayed in a room next to him. In their conversation, he learned about the excitement of the carnival that took place in town. He was aware of that carnival. However, due to his job, he had not yet had the opportunity to attend it.

Hope paid for his room and took care of his daily needs. He had barely enough extra money to spare. Of course, he was also aware that once he left the mission house, he could not go back to stay there again.

Gloomy as the next day looked, he was not overly worried about what might happen the following day. Hope was learning to take life one day at a time. That had been the case for him in the recent past. He believed his needs would be met somehow. How that would happen he did not know. Before long, he was fast asleep.

Hope woke up the next morning well rested. He took a shower and made up his bed. He felt a strong urge to go to the carnival. However, he could not make up his mind whether he should or not. He toyed with the idea of doing something else to while away the time.

No matter how strongly he resisted the temptation of attending the carnival, the urge to do so only grew. Ultimately, it got the better of him. He recounted the money he had in his pocket and thought how best to use it. At that point, he heard a knock on his door. It was his uncompromising property owner. He gave Hope the choice: a payment in full for the next day's rent or moving out by noon.

Hope, therefore, left as his property owner requested with no definite place to go. He wandered in the neighborhood for a while in hopes that he might find a cheaper place or stumble on another halfway house that might take him in. He opted to follow his instinct to go to the carnival. After the carnival, he intended to find a hiding place to catch a night's sleep and then continue to take one day at a time.

He was by now familiar with the bus routes. So he got on the public bus and made his way to the carnival. This was the first time he had attended a carnival. All alone, he went from stand to stand. He looked at the numerous items on display at each stand. When he got to a certain stand, he saw a young fellow about his age win an item.

Hope was tempted to try his hand at winning one of the items. It occurred to him that he would have no place to keep that item if he won it. Thus, he gave up on that idea and moved on to the next stands.

He saw a group of people at one of the nearby stands and was curious to ascertain what the center of attraction there was. When he drew nearer to the stand, he saw the prettiest of exotic and mesmerizing colorful glass items on display.

CHAPTER

11

From the Unreal to Reality

Floretta, a strikingly beautiful girl of eighteen, lived with her parents in the suburbs of Giboad City. Her family belonged to the middle-class income group. Her father, Barry Pritchard, had worked twenty years as a welder and supervisor at Senecan Manufacturing Company. Her mother, Irene, was a tailor. Floretta was the only child of her parents.

People who were familiar with her family considered her a spoiled young woman because she got virtually everything she asked of them. The word around town was that she was born prematurely at Belvac Teaching Hospital. Her chances for survival at birth were slim to none. That was probably the reason why she got the royal treatment. However, those closest to her family knew of another highly guarded reason why they continually pampered her.

By divine grace, she beat the odds and survived for eighteen years. So noticeable was her beauty that many believed she was an angel who sojourned on earth to manifest the exquisite handiwork of the Divine Creator! She stood five feet eight inches tall. She had an immaculate set of pearly permanent teeth, which were strikingly noticeable each time she gave her unique dazzling smile. Her silky black hair ran down her shoulders.

As the daughter of a tailor, she wore many fine, fashionable clothes. Her ivory smooth skin glittered from the subtle rays of the early morning sun as she walked her dogs along the sidewalk of her neighborhood. Despite her gorgeous looks and earthly possessions, she was a humble, kind-natured young woman. She was a loner. Although she had briefly dated a couple of people, she was still a virgin.

Beula and Estella were identical twins who lived in the same neighborhood as Floretta. They attended the same high school and graduated together. They often tried to get close to Floretta. However, each of their efforts met with little or no success.

On her eighteenth birthday, Floretta received a beautiful, uniquely designed flower vase from her parents. That was what she asked for. She also received an African violet seedling from her teacher for being the best student in interior decoration when she graduated from high school. She valued both the flower vase and plant so much that she kept them at her bedside.

One night, she had a bad dream. In that dream, she saw someone who tried to steal her flower vase. She struggled fiercely with that person. During the course of that struggle, the vase fell and broke into seven pieces. As she sat on her bed and cried her heart out, a strange but handsome young man handed her a replacement vase of the same type.

Floretta suddenly woke up from her dream. Desperate to verify that it was only a dream, she reached out her right hand to ensure that the real vase was still intact. Since she was still half-asleep, she caught hold of the vase at the wrong side and actually dropped it on the tiled floor in her room. It broke into seven pieces just as she had seen in her dream. She was heartbroken and disappointed.

Floretta was the most upset of all girls in the wide world after that mishap. She did not know how to explain what happened to her parents. If only she could secretly find out where they had bought it for her, she would save part of her pocket money to get it replaced as soon as she could.

That morning it was obvious to Floretta's parents that she was not quite herself. She had a strange look on her face that told the story of a shattered, battered beauty who experienced the agony of defeat. Her parents tried to learn the cause of her sadness. However, she made it clear to her parents she wanted to be left alone. Later that afternoon, she rode her bicycle to their neighborhood park to get over her frustrations.

The loss of the vase had a major impact on her emotions. Anyone who saw her riding her bicycle noticed that she was not the same charming congenial neighborhood beauty.

At the park, she took a seat in the shade of one of the oak trees and watched the children play. Some people were at the park for a picnic. Others flew kites with their kids. The others were there for a good time, but not Floretta, the beauty of beauties.

Beula and Estella happened to be at the park as well. They intended to go to the carnival after they left the park. They saw Floretta sitting all alone under the shade of one of the oak trees. They could not believe their eyes. That was unlike her. She rarely ventured outside her home by herself.

The twin sisters at first meant to ignore her since she was previously not receptive to their friendly gestures. However, on second thought, they reasoned that this might be another chance to break into the lonely life of their beautiful, reclusive neighbor.

"Hi, Floretta. What's happening?" Beula asked.

"Oh well, a little bit of everything," she answered drily.

"What are you doing sitting here by yourself? Come on and join us," Estella requested. "We are taking a stroll to the pond to feed the geese. It's a lot of fun."

"Uh! I do not … Can I think about it? Well, I guess that will be okay," Floretta agreed.

"Have you heard about the carnival in town?" Beula said. "Wow, everyone is talking about it. I mean, everyone who was there thinks it is fantastic. We are planning to be there this evening. Would you mind coming with us? Hey, remember, we are neighbors, and it would be nice for all of us to get together and do things girls in a neighborhood do together while they are still young. After a while, we might grow up, get married, and go our separate ways. You know what I mean?"

Floretta maintained that same funny look on her face. It was as if she was not too sure, whether she should go with them to the carnival. "I would have to ask my parents about that," she replied. "They may have some other plans that I am not aware of."

"Go ahead, friend, and talk it over with your parents. Let us know something by six p.m. We can come by and pick you up. Peace!" they both added with a smile.

Floretta's parents agreed to let her go to the carnival with her neighborhood friends. She called to inform them accordingly. At six p.m. on the dot, the three young girls left for the carnival. At the carnival, they saw a variety of activities that tickled their fancy. They went from stand to stand. Then suddenly something got Floretta's attention.

At one of the stands decorated with red, gold and blue banners, she saw the same type of flower vase that she once had. The booth's attendant had placed it at the middle of other glass and chinaware. It revolved on a small pedestal. To win any item from that stand, one must purchase a token from the operator of that stand. The purchaser must successfully hurl the purchased token from a demarcated distance on the items on display. If the token successfully got inside an item, the contestant automatically won that particular item on display.

Floretta stood still, gazing pensively at the vase. She was so mesmerized at the sight of the vase that she could not hear when her companions asked what was amiss. She vividly recalled the dream she'd had the night before. Right before her eyes was the same type of vase she would do almost anything to secure as replacement for the one broken in her room. She could win it with an accurate throw of a token. She could literally feel tingling vibrations and action potentials that traveled from her cerebral cortex to the cerebellum.

She mapped out the trajectory of the token, as she built more and more confidence in her ability to hurl it into the vase. She almost broke out in a cold sweat when she learned this was the last night of the carnival. She needed to do something before someone else won that vase.

She hurriedly looked into her purse to purchase the required token, but alas! She had left her pocketbook on her dresser as she quickly got ready to leave with her friends to the carnival. She asked her friends to lend her some money. Between them, they came up with the amount Floretta needed to purchase seven tokens from the operator of that stand. That was necessary win for her.

She aimed and threw her first five tokens but missed her target by wide margins. Her friends encouraged her to keep trying. The sixth token she threw fell into an ashtray. She had only one token left. She was so tensed up that the sweat from her brow appeared like drops of blood streaming down her face.

She stared at her friends for more support. She took in deep breaths to calm herself. Should she or should she not throw in her last token? At last, she summoned enough courage to throw her last token into the vase.

Incidentally, Hope arrived just then at that same stand. He carefully and keenly observed all that was going on at that stand. Namely, a beautiful, elegant young woman was trying to win a beautiful flower vase, seemingly in vain. Floretta continued to formulate a strategy on how to make her last throw. That aroused Hope's interest in that vase. He considered trying his luck at winning it anyway, just for the fun of it.

Floretta's anxiety level shot sky-high when she noticed she had a competitor. The two hemispheres of her brain were on a collision course with each other. The left hemisphere strived to control activities of the right side of her body, while the right hemisphere moved at the peak of its physiological endowment to control activities of the left side of her body. It was such a tense, quiet moment that one could hear the drop of a needle on a haystack!

Finally, she hurled her last token in hopes that it would land inside the flower vase she had her eyes on. The token hit the edge of the vase and bounced off.

Hope's very first attempt fell right inside the vase. Floretta nearly dropped dead when she saw Hope's token fall into the vase she badly wanted to win. Tears ran down her cheeks. For once, she felt she was a loser. A loser in life, or was she a victim of circumstances? She stood astounded with her mouth wide open in disbelief. They knew she could not stay around to see Hope receive the vase from the operator of that stand.

Hope held the vase tightly with both of his hands. He saw Floretta look helplessly at the vase he held firmly in his hands. She was disappointed. Very disappointed. As their eyes met, it occurred to Hope that he had nowhere to keep that vase. He was convinced that young pretty woman who tried her very best to win that vase needed it more than he did. He took a good look at Floretta, boldly walked up to her, and said, "Well, pretty lady, I thought you'd like to have this vase. I hate the look of disappointment on your face. This might cheer you up."

The unexpected move Hope made amazed both Floretta and her companions. She was speechless for a moment. In a flash, she remembered the latter part of her dream. She could not believe what she heard. At first, she acted as if she did not want to accept such a gift from a stranger.

However, she could not resist the applause and cheers of encouragement she received from her friends and other bystanders. As soon as she received the vase, Hope turned around and walked away. However, something deep within Floretta prompted her to act courageously and call him back.

"Sir, you did not even give me the opportunity to thank you for this priceless gift," she said. "I will always cherish this. I will never forget this day. I would also like to express my thanks to these two sisters who suggested that I accompany them to this carnival. I will definitely tell my parents about what has happened."

"I am glad you do like it. It was my pleasure to present it to you," Hope replied.

"I don't even know your name." she said.

"Hope," he answered.

"That's an unusual name. It has a ring to it," she remarked.

"Seriously speaking, that's my real name," responded Hope.

"You must be passing through town," Beula said, making it a question.

"How do you know that, or was it a lucky guess?" he asked.

"There's something different about you. I can't quite put my finger on it. I've moved around this part of town quite a bit, and you don't look familiar," she said.

"Maybe I'm a special person. It is very interesting to learn that you have a photographic memory," remarked Hope.

"I was on the women's basketball team. My sister and I are members of several youth organizations around here. As such we get to go to quite a few places in town."

"Great. Then you'd be able to furnish me with information I need," said Hope.

"What kind of information do you need, pretty boy?" asked Estella.

"Information about where to stay and where to look for a job," said Hope.

"Talk to the lady with the flower vase," said Beula. "Her father might be able to help you with part of that."

Floretta smiled. Hope thought she was shy by nature. After a lengthy conversation, Hope convinced them that he desperately and genuinely needed a job and a place to stay. They were sympathetic to his plight, especially Floretta, who listened attentively to him, though she did not have much to say.

"There is a cheap motel near where we live. They have very reasonable prices. We can take you there, if you'd like," suggested Floretta.

"I would like to, but—"

Floretta suspected from Hope's facial expression that he probably did not have enough money on him to pay for the motel. However, to avoid any embarrassment, she was hesitant for a moment. Then she said, "Come with us anyway. There is nothing wrong with returning your kindness. We might be able to come up with something."

The small kindness Hope showed to Floretta had a major impact on her. She felt very comfortable with him. She did not seem to have any negative vibrations about him. Although he was unaware of it, she had two things on her mind.

First, if it turned out that Hope did not really have enough money on him, then she would supplement whatever he had from the money she had set aside to replace her broken vase or if possible, she would ask her parents if Hope could stay in their guest quarters for that night.

It might seem a little awkward for her to bring a stranger home the first time she went out to town with her friends. She pondered how her parents would interpret that. Nevertheless, she was convinced that either way, she would have done the right thing. Beula and Estella also offered assistance if Floretta's parents were uncooperative.

Beneath her strong conviction was a mild feeling of uncertainty about how her mother would react to her request.

She looked at her friends with concern. She knew quite well that her mother might hold them responsible for the 'genesis of the tale of blasphemy' that might crop up in the minds of her parents. She chose to go ahead with her gut feelings anyway, in hopes that truth would always stand. Truth had never failed anyone. Truth knew no peers or boundaries. Truth was as sharp as a two-edged sword that could clearly cut between right and wrong. The truth was the banner of the righteous.

Meanwhile, Floretta's parents anxiously awaited her return home from the carnival. They looked at the wall clock in their living room every five minutes in anticipation of her return.

Suddenly, they heard a car stop in front of their house. Her mother quickly turned on the front porch light. It was Floretta, and right behind her was a young man who stood about six-foot-three and probably weighed 220 pounds.

She could not believe her eyes. Thus, she asked her husband to open the front door. Actually, she wanted him to see the unexpected reality for himself, since he was instrumental in allowing Floretta to go to the carnival with her neighbors.

"What's the matter?" he asked. "Is something wrong?"

"Not a thing. I only wanted you to see the fruit of your decision to let her go out on her own."

"Hi Dad, Mom. I want you to meet Hope. We met him at the carnival. He helped me at the carnival. He is a good person but a stranger in town. He needs help desperately. I realize that this is an impromptu meeting, but I think Dad can be of help to him. That's why I brought him home," she explained to her parents.

"Good evening. It is nice to meet you," responded Barry as he shook Hope's hand.

"How do you do, young man?" her mother added. "Have a seat right there."

Floretta explained Hope's situation to her parents. Her father was very sympathetic to Hope's plight. Her mother was more inquisitive. However, due to the kind reception given Hope by her husband, she supported the idea that Floretta should call the nearby cheap motel to verify if they had any vacancies.

As it turned out, they were booked solid that night due to the carnival and convention in town. Floretta asked her parents if Hope could spend the night in their guest quarters, to give them time to sort things out. They granted her request. Truly, Floretta got whatever she wanted from her parents.

Hope was very pleased but nervous. Since Hope was tired from the activities of the day, he asked to be excused to go to bed early. He refused an offer for a snack before retiring to bed.

After Hope went to bed, Floretta recounted her dream and the actual loss of her flower vase to her parents. That was the overwhelming reason she felt the finger of God was in that situation. After they heard the entire story, her parents also became comfortable with Hope and did not ask further probing questions about him. Neither did they entertain an iota of doubt about her motives.

Floretta could not get Hope out of her mind that night. She stayed wide awake throughout that night. The dream she previously had played repeatedly in her mind. She compared and contrasted the details of that dream to what actually happened that day. All the time she was lonely, extremely lonely.

She focused her attention on Hope. It progressed from a mere dream, to Hope actually presenting a flower vase to her. Hope incidentally fit the description of the man she saw in her dream.

She was glad to have returned Hope's kindness to her. The more she thought about the entire development, the more she was convinced it was no mere coincidence. No matter how hard she tried to dismiss that thought, the more it played back in her mind. Things steadily moved from a state of imagination to visualization.

As was always the case, Nature has a way of lulling a wandering mind to sleep eventually. Even though it lasted only a few hours, Floretta slept soundly and deeply in the early morning hours.

She did such a fantastic job in presenting Hope's plight to her parents that during that night while she was asleep, they decided to do more to help him above what she expected.

She was the first to get up the next morning. At breakfast, they got to know their special guest a little better. They invited Hope to stay with them for a few more days while Barry helped him find a job in town.

CHAPTER

12

Paving the Road to Happiness

Barry brought Hope an employment application from Senecan Manufacturing Company, where he worked. He had inside information that the employment office planned to hire additional employees. Therefore, he wanted Hope to have a head start in the application process.

At the fullness of time, they notified Hope he was among candidates selected for a job interview. Hope performed well at the interview. However, he was not hired for the position. He did not have the required experience for the job. Despite that setback, Hope was not discouraged. On his way to the interview, he saw several factories near Senecan Manufacturing Company.

During their conversation in the car, on their way to that interview, Barry casually mentioned to him a couple of vacancies might come up at a bigger conglomerate called CHIG in that industrial area. He intended to keep his ears opened for further details. He promised to pass further details to Hope as they became available.

Later that night, alone in the guest quarters of the Pritchard residence, Hope reflected on the new developments in his life. He was in a desperate situation. He took seriously Barry's information regarding CHIG. To him it was an opportunity to take charge of his destiny. Whether the events that took place in his life thus far could be attributed to fate, destiny, or divine purpose he did not know. However, the fact remained: no matter what it was, he had made it thus far in his quest to rise above life's challenges.

Though he did not know how long he could stay with the Pritchards, he felt he was at the crossroads of life. He knew he needed to act fast without wavering in his resolve to attain his goals. Certainly, he was alert and sensitive to the real possibility that CHIG presented an opportunity that must be seized. If he was able to do that, he might be on track for success. If he did not, there was a possibility that additional chances for success might either diminish or never come by him again; or he could become complacent with the status quo.

He had cried out in his own way for mercy and compassion from strangers since his arrival at Giboad City. Even though he did not have perfect knowledge about CHIG, he believed Barry's casual information about two opportunities that might come up at CHIG. In his voracious readings to preoccupy him during his trials in Avenice, Hope recalled a story about eagles atop tall trees, where they made their nests. They had learned to discern the various winds that blew. They could distinguish between the appropriate wind currents they could use to soar to a desired location. That lesson from the eagle stirred him to follow up on the CHIG lead.

He had enough intuitive acumen to realize that he could not allow someone else to make that move for him. It was something he must do by himself. He was motivated to be persistent and not waver even in the face of opposition.

To reinforce his decision, he additionally recalled a conversation he'd heard during his childhood between his late dad and a retired former employee of one of the aerospace companies in Avenice. That retired employee provided an explanation of how an aircraft obtained their lift force from the runway during takeoff. The control tower operators directed the pilot to take off from a specific runway. The operator knew the wind direction at that runway. If his memory served him right, the force of the wind blowing against the aircraft provided the force to get off the ground. Thus, the take-home lesson he drew from that story was that oppositions could be good if we learned how to use them to our advantage.

He drew on that story. He was determined not to waver whenever he faced opposition. Like an aircraft that flew into the opposing wind, he too might get the needed push to rise above the uncertainties of life. That required persistence. If he followed that resolution, he hoped to develop endurance, a necessary component of the dynamism of hope.

Finally, he must set high goals for himself. CHIG to him symbolized that great goal he needed to circumvent. Even though he did not have perfect knowledge about the company culture of CHIG or additional details about the rumored upcoming positions, he felt that he must act right away.

Based on his mental deliberations, Hope suggested to Barry to drop him off at the industrial area on his way to work the following morning so that he could continue his job search.

He went from one company to another to complete employment applications. By three p.m. he was exhausted. However, he had an inkling to complete yet one more application. Barry would pick him up on his way home from work around 5:15 p.m. at a predetermined place. Therefore, he had enough time to do that.

Hope continued his job search east of the industrial area. He saw a huge sign in front of a massive industrial complex that read, "Crystal Horizon Industrial Group." Suddenly, there it was, the huge company Barry referred to as CHIG. He decided to go there. At the plant entrance, Hope quickly discovered that there was a security guard shack through which all personnel must pass.

As he entered the guard shack, one of the security guards confronted him and demanded proof of the reason for his visit to the human resources office. He did not have any. It was around shift change. The security guard on duty asked him to go through the exit door. He encouraged him to return when he had a valid reason for a subsequent visit to that facility. Nevertheless, Hope insisted on speaking to the head of human resources. Finally, almost at the point of no return, he dropped Barry's name to the security guard.

"You mean Barry Pritchard at Senecan sent you here?" the security guard asked.

"He said it would be worthwhile to speak to the head of human resources," responded Hope.

"Why did he not call or give you a note to see her? Does she know about this?"

"I did not ask him for details," Hope answered.

"Barry is well known around here," said the security guard. "However, we cannot allow just anyone from the street to enter this facility based on hearsay. Let me check a couple of things first. I don't even know whether she is still in her office."

Hope was not about to back down from his insistence on seeing the head of human resources, even if that meant he must take a risk. He went on the information Barry gave him. Even though it could be considered hearsay, he followed up on that lead. Hope did not believe Barry would lie to him about something that important. He was anxious to get a head start before the positions were officially advertised, but he could not relay that to the security guard.

Though he ran into opposition, Hope did not lose hope. He had the will to stand his ground. He did not allow himself to slip into the doldrums of sadness, discouragement, and despair. He was convinced he had a real opportunity to put in an employment application at CHIG.

He had other reasons to stand his ground. He wanted to disprove a statement that haunted him. Jimmy characterized him as a good-for-nothing young man. He wanted to prove him wrong.

His failure could mean the loss of the opportunity to eventually rescue Avenice from its economic decadence, redeem his family name, develop a viable profession for himself, and make his life meaningful as well as purposeful. Thus, there was a lot at stake as far as he was concerned. Hope considered such factors integral components of the purpose of his destiny.

He stood at the crossroads and was determined to persist to victory no matter how miniscule the opportunity that presented itself.

There were anxious moments as he faced the security guard. He watched the guard make a few calls, presumably to the head of human resources or Barry to verify his statement. For some reason, none of those calls went through. Hope slipped into a pensive meditative state shortly. In order for him to gain access to the head of human resources at CHIG, something miraculous must happen.

At that point, someone tapped on his shoulder. It was Quincy Baah, the security guard he previously met at the rail terminal on his first arrival at Giboad City. It was Quincy who had given him a ride to the mission house where he lodged for a few days. The security company he worked for also provided security services to CHIG. He recognized Hope and told the other security guard that he would take care of this situation. Thus, Hope got the miracle he asked, sought, and knocked on the heavenly realm for.

Quincy asked him to take a seat as he went through procedures to relieve the guard who had tried to prevent Hope from going to the human resources office. A situation that could have been disastrous to Hope's purpose turned out to be an opportunity for them to get reacquainted since they last saw each other.

Hope related how desperate he was to get employment at CHIG despite the opposition he ran into with the previous security guard. He had heard through the grapevine that a couple of openings might come up soon. However, he did not have any inside connections.

Quincy paused for a moment, and then told Hope, "Wait a minute, friend. I got into a conversation with the head of human resources about three days ago. If my memory serves me right, I heard her say she was born and raised at a town near Avenice. However, they had to relocate here. Is that where you told me you were from?"

"It is a small world. Yes, that is my hometown, Avenice," replied Hope.

"Well, in that case she might be your in to CHIG. Let me call her office and see if she has not left work yet," he said.

"That will be great. Give her a shout, buddy." Hope was already excited.

"She is still there in her office. She said she was about to leave but can squeeze in a few minutes to talk to you. Go down that hallway there. Take the first turn to the left. She is in Room 215. Good luck, friend," Quincy said.

"I don't know how to thank you for this great chance you have given me. I owe you one," responded Hope as he hurried down the hallway.

Within a couple of minutes, he got into the office of the head of human resources at CHIG. She was a middle-aged woman. She was about five foot eight inches tall, bespectacled, well-groomed, and adorned with a variety of jewelry.

"Hello there. Have a seat. I am happy to see you. My name is Tina, Tina Doyer, Here is my business card. Quincy, the security guard, told me you were from Avenice. Is that right?"

"Yes, that is correct. I appreciate your kindness by making time to visit with me," said Hope as he gave her a firm handshake.

"No problem. What's your name?"

"Hope. Hope De Pinto."

"Come again?" she said.

"Hope De Pinto," he responded.

"That name rings a bell. You look familiar. Are you sure we never met somewhere before?" she asked.

"I don't think so. As a matter of fact, I was surprised to learn you were from the Avenice area."

"What brought you to Giboad City, if I may ask?"

"I am a victim of circumstances. Looking for an opportunity to turn things around. This is where fate or destiny has brought me. I am desperately looking for work. I heard there might be a couple of openings coming up here. I would appreciate the opportunity to be considered for employment here," he said.

"How did you, a stranger find out about the available positions that might be coming up?" she asked. "We normally hire candidates for employment through an agency, you know."

"I met a young lady called Floretta at the carnival. She was kind enough to introduce me to her parents. In fact, one thing led to another, and I am staying with them right now," he responded.

"What is the name of this family who opened their home to you, if I may ask that as well?" she inquired.

"Floretta's father is Barry Pritchard. He is a supervisor at Senecan Manufacturing. His wife, Irene, is a seamstress."

"Oh, Barry Pritchard. Barry is a good man. I listened to my voice messages and heard that he called. However, I have not had the chance to return his call. What is your level of education? Where else have you tried to seek employment?"

"I am a high school graduate with big dreams. I know I am capable of soaring to great heights if given the opportunity. Since my arrival I worked at a downtown restaurant to make ends meet."

"What is the name of that restaurant?"

"Archway Palace," he replied.

"The Archway Palace? That is our favorite hangout. Now, wait a minute. I knew you looked familiar. Were you the server who wasted a bowl of salad on me the other night?" she asked curiously.

Hope paused for a moment. He looked intensely at Tina. He thought he had put that incident behind him. However, it seemed to have reared its ugly head once again in his path. A potential misfortune threatened to derail the real opportunity he thought he had at gaining permanent employment at CHIG.

"Oh, now I remember you. I was sorry for what happened. I still am sorry for what happened. If I could take it back, I would. I don't know what else to say," he responded.

"Don't worry about it. My husband had a bad day, and I think he overreacted. I will not hold that against you. It is water under the bridge right now. I would like to go back to our conversation regarding Avenice. You said your name was Hope De Pinto?"

"Yes, that's correct."

"The De Pintos were very prominent in Avenice. Would you happen to know of one Edmund De Pinto?"

"Yes, that was my dad," said Hope.

"Okay, I knew you looked familiar. I knew Edmund very well. I heard that he died at sea?"

"Yes and my life has never been the same."

"Well, going back to the positions you mentioned, it is true they will be coming up," she said. "One of them requires a degree. The other is an entry-level position. However, the successful candidate will have the opportunity to pursue a degree program at a local university, and we will pay for it as part of our benefits program. It looks like you might be a good candidate for that position. Let us see what we can do to help you, young man. Complete this application form and bring it back. I will be in touch with you, soon after I get it back from you. Here is my card. If the security guard queries you, show it to him."

Hope left her office with mixed emotions. Nevertheless, something deep within caused him to believe that he had a good chance at securing that entry-level position.

As he walked out of Tina's office, he realized it was almost time for Barry to pick him up. He shared with Barry all that happened to him that day, especially at CHIG. Barry felt Hope was a risk-taker. He, however, he should have informed him of his surprise visit to the CHIG plant. He was happy he had left Tina a voice message in advance . It was their hope and expectation that Hope's dreams would materialize.

Tina returned Barry's call the following day. True to her word, she had private conversations with others in key positions at CHIG. She was able to pull many strings behind the scenes to get Hope that position they privately discussed after he went through the formal application process. His efforts paid off.

Hope continued to stay with the Pritchard family until he got his first paycheck. He subsequently moved into a small but nice neighborhood garage apartment. He continued to visit Floretta and her parents from time to time. After a few weeks of occasional visits, and casual phone calls, his friendship with Floretta slowly developed into proportions that were more serious.

During that transitional period, Hope took driving lessons and obtained a driver's license. A neighborhood widow had had a good working car parked in her garage for quite some time. Her late husband took meticulous care of it while he was alive. Her children were in the process of putting her in a retirement home. She had a garage sale and sold that car at rock-bottom price to Hope.

Hope and Floretta enjoyed each other's company and got along very well. So gentle did Hope appear to both Floretta and her parents that one evening Hope asked her out on a date. That invitation met with no resistance even from her mother, as long as she returned home at a decent hour. That meant she had to be back at home before midnight.

Hope and Floretta went to watch a movie that evening. Floretta selected the movie. After the movie, they stopped by a fast-food restaurant and then went to Hope's apartment to chat for a while. Hope was a teetotaler. However, he had good taste in music. Although his garage apartment was small, he had it well decorated and homey.

He put on some soft music and dimmed the lights. He asked Floretta to dance with him. However, it was obvious that a lot went through both of their minds. After a couple of dances, they sat down in his love seat. Suddenly, Hope seemed restless. He got up and walked to the window to the east of his apartment.

Then he came back to sit closely beside her. They gazed at each other straight in the eyes. They held hands and expressed how much they cared for each other.

As if it was an afterthought, Floretta backed off, and said to Hope, "I think I should be going home. It is getting close to midnight."

"Oh! I know. You have to be home by midnight."

"This is our first real date. We can't mess things up."

"Certainly, I do understand," said Hope. "It is just a matter of time. You know, time can do so much, as they say, right?"

"That's right. I like that one thing about you. You are such an understanding man. I am learning to trust you more and more. I hope we continue to get closer and closer than we are now. It all started at a carnival. Now look where we are. Isn't that something?"

"Yeah, I definitely hope so, too. I see no reason why we can't."

"We had a wonderful time tonight, didn't we?" she asked.

"I enjoyed every bit of it."

"I think I should be leaving now."

"Well then, let me get my keys and take you home," he responded.

He took her home. After a brief embrace, she walked into the house and waved goodbye.

Hope had left home primarily because it was obvious he was trapped in a mud of frustration in Avenice. His whole world seemed to have crumbled and come to a grinding and dismal halt after the death of his dad and the appearance of Jimmy into Charlotte's life. He needed to wipe off that slippery mud of despair finally.

He needed to make necessary adjustments in his quality of life. He must embark on a new direction. A direction that might take him to a higher and more fertile ground so that he could get a better traction on the narrow road to success and happiness.

After all that had happened thus far, he felt the tide had moved in his favor. Giboad City seemed to be that drier ground where he could systematically wipe off the mud of hopelessness and despair.

However, even on that higher, drier ground, as he would soon discover, some of the mud remained between his toes. Each time he was lonely or whenever something or someone got him upset, he experienced occasional flashbacks to those agonizing days in Avenice.

During such flashback episodes, Hope stood in front of his bathroom mirror and saw his pupils dilated. He experienced a rise in his blood pressure and heart rate; he could literally feel an increase in glucose-rich blood flow throughout his body. Yes, he could visualize his adipose cells breaking down fat to increase available energy in his body.

When those sensations threatened to overwhelm him, especially on his job, Hope did his best to maintain his composure. He knew what he had gone through before he got his current job. He clearly understood the opportunities for advancement that lay ahead of him. He was determined to do whatever it took to keep his job under all circumstances.

Floretta proved to be a comforting source of support and encouragement. He learned to depend on her as a friend. Her patience, her undivided attention when he shared his problems with her, her understanding and love were priceless. Those attributes she exuded formed a solid basis of his love and admiration for her.

One Friday night, while alone in his apartment, Hope continued to reflect on his life. He turned off his phone in order not to be disturbed. So far, his determination to overcome his obstacles, diligent efforts to be sensitive to changing circumstances, careful and timely planning, and his strong faith in the divine Creator had enabled him to keep his head above water. The Creator mysteriously worked behind the scenes to intervene in the affairs of those who placed their unwavering trust in Him, and His timely intervention helped Hope ride the waves associated with the uncertainties of life.

Hope recalled some of his conversations with counterparts at the youth center in Avenice and at the mission house in Giboad City. He also had many talks about life with his colleagues at work. He concluded that problems in life, no matter their origin or the way they presented themselves to people, were not entirely new to humankind. Others had experienced similar problems and found a way to overcome them.

Hope made another startling discovery. He recalled that from the time he first arrived in Giboad City up until the time he moved out to stay on his own, his preoccupation and focus on survival had helped him to suppress the issues that caused him to leave home in Avenice. He discovered that most of life's battles raged in his mind. He needed to find a way to develop mental toughness.

He did not run away from the issues that stared at him wherever and however he tried to avoid them. Neither was he a fugitive. Previously, he had relied on people, events, and objects to overcome his frustrations, disappointments, and stagnations at various dimensions of his well-being. He discovered that those were useful but temporary aids to the solution of his problems.

What he needed under those circumstances were time and space for himself. They had proven to be key elements to steer him from the broad path of decadence and despair in a hopeless situation to an alternate direction that led him in a timely manner to develop a will and subsequent way to win back his self-confidence and victory.

Another thing Hope did was to channel the negative energies of his previous experiences in Avenice to more positive and innovative acts in Giboad City. Recognition of that awareness energized him the more. It motivated him to cultivate sustained hope that he was convinced would one day make him a *victor*, not a *victim* of circumstances.

Aside from his other attributes, Hope was a gifted artist. He spent part of his available time painting. Before long, he had a number of colorful artworks, a couple of which he gave to Floretta. Slowly but surely, Hope filled in the empty or idle voids that cropped up in his mind periodically with a variety of good things that kept him in great spirits most of the time.

He looked at the bright side of life. As for those whose deliberate or unintentional actions previously kept him upset, he resolved to respond to them with a smile. He learned to forgive them in his heart.

Hope was exhausted and fell asleep. Once again, he had a vivid dream. He saw the image of the same man who he assumed was his late dad, Edmund. In this dream the man stood on a hill. In his right hand he held the same silver coin as in the previous dreams. He summoned Hope to come up where he stood.

On his way up to meet the man, Hope fell down a few times. However, he did not stay down when he fell. He drew upon an inner strength and got up to continue his climb toward the man. Eventually he made it to the top of the hill where the man stood. The man looked at him in a congratulatory way with a smile on his face. He then offered Hope the silver coin.

However, six times Hope tried to receive it, and six times a thick, glassy, transparent, yet firm curtain separated his hand from that of the man. On his seventh attempt, Hope felt he had the chance to break through the curtain and receive the coin. He got a chance to really take a closer look at the man who gave him the silver coin. He wanted to ensure that he really was his late father, Edmund. Just then, he woke up. He had to attend to nature's call. It was an untimely interruption of his dream, as far as Hope was concerned.

Hope wondered if that was one of the resolutions he recently made. Alternatively, could it be a premonition that he was on the right path to a long-awaited victory? True to his word, he looked at the bright side of the dream. He wrote a poem on an index card, which he pinned on the wall in his bedroom. It read:

> Positive thinking gives Encouragement.
> Encouragement subdues Disappointment.
> Subdued Disappointment nurtures Determination.
> Sustained Determination, Personal Effort, and Perseverance
> Will ultimately lead to the Path of
> Success in the Fullness of Time.

The following morning Hope called Floretta to ask if she had any plans for that day. He invited her to have lunch with him. He did his weekly housecleaning activities and left for the grocery store to pick up a few items to prepare lunch for the two of them.

He prepared a particular seafood dish he knew she liked. Right at the time he got through preparing that dish, she called to inform him she was on her way to join him.

She entered his apartment, which had at that time become a routine hideaway for her at various times during the week. She complimented him on the neat and orderly appearance of his apartment, as usual. She could smell the food he had prepared and knew exactly what it was.

"You amaze me by the way you keep this place spotless for a young bachelor," she remarked.

"Thank you," he responded. "I do my best to remain neat. That is important; it's one of the values instilled in me as a kid growing up."

"Most young men like you seldom find time to keep their apartments or houses clean. My friends tell me that their dates are usually preoccupied with other things they must do."

"That's true to some extent. I think people have the choice to plan for whatever they want to do. It depends also on the manner in which they were raised."

"I smell something nice," she said. "It appears you prepared my favorite dish once again, huh?"

"Yes, I did. I knew that would be a pleasant surprise to you. The recipe is all mine. I plan to modify it in the future so that it won't be a stereotyped dish."

"I told my mom about that the first time you prepared it. She wanted me to get the recipe from you."

"I'll give it to you whenever you want," he said. "Are you ready to eat? I am starving."

"Yes, I am."

After lunch, the lovely Floretta made a remark that caught Hope by surprise. "There is something different about you today."

"What do you mean, darling?"

"I noticed a drastic change in your mood. You seem to have a different attitude. You are calmer, happier, and more positive. Your actions and expressions are quite different from the way they used to be. Don't get me wrong. You have always been a nice man. However, there is something different, different about you. It shows. I wonder what brought about this change."

"I'm still the same man you've always known," he responded. "Handsome, caring, loving, and attentive, with a desire to keep you number one in my life. What else can I say?"

"Are you bragging about yourself?"

"Of course not. I'm just trying to read your mind."

"I don't mean your attitude toward me per se," she said. "You appear to be a much happier person today. Yes, I know you are always happy whenever I am with you. It's hard to explain the change I see in you. It is like your inner spirit has been uplifted to a higher plane."

Hope sat quietly for a moment. Then he told her about his recent resolutions.

"I made some important decisions early this morning. That's what I'm going to pursue from now on," he began.

"What did you decide to do? I'm certainly interested in knowing what is coming down the pipe, so to speak."

"I've taken stock of my life. I know where I was. In addition, I know where I would like to be. I have taken the good with the bad and come up with a new recipe for the direction of my life. That includes taking advantage of a scholarship program at CHIG to complete my college education. Does that surprise you?"

"Not really," she replied. "I know you are very smart, based on my interactions with you, as well as seeing your interactions with others. I feel deep within my bones that you will make it if you try."

"That's very supportive of you. I'll keep that in mind."

"By the way, how does the college scholarship fit in with your current job? Are you going to have time for your job and academic requirements, and do well on your grades?"

"It's not going to be easy. However, I have thought through it all," he responded. "I can maintain a focus on both. CHIG made a business decision to invest in its employees. All I have to do is complete a few forms and submit them to the human resources department. They will pay for my fees as long as I maintain at least a B average. I will be promoted after I complete my degree. There is opportunity for growth with CHIG. They see great potential in me for their long-range goals. Don't forget, I have you as my cheerleader. You've done a great job at that so far!"

Floretta paused for a moment, sinking into a pensive mood. Then suddenly she asked him, "With you holding a full-time job and attending school, I see no chance of you having adequate time for me, as you now do."

"You have nothing to worry about. I just got through telling you that with careful planning one can always find time for whatever one desires to do."

"Yeah. I hope you do not change. Some people change when they begin to make progress. I hope you keep in mind the relationship we have built together. I love you, Hope."

"Come on, babe. With me, what you see is what you get," he said. "I meant it when I told you I loved you. I will not play with you like that.

"This is an opportunity for us to talk a bit more about the future. It would be a good idea to find out more about each other—don't you think so?"

"Oh yes, I agree with you about that," she replied. "My background is not all that exciting anyway. Is there anything in particular you would like to know?"

"Nothing really. However, I do not think it will be a bad idea for you to give me a detailed rundown of your family background. Things have moved rather quickly between us. I do not want you to get the wrong impression that I am looking for a perfect woman. No one is perfect. We all have our good and bad sides. You see, too many people these days rush into marriage for trivial reasons. You know what I mean. Then, shortly thereafter, they realize they did the wrong thing. I personally believe there is more to marriage than meets the eye. Don't you?"

"I agree. Let me say that I am very proud of you for the way you think about something as sacred as marriage. It is also important to ensure that we are really in love, have common interests and ideals, and have a good understanding of each other. It is better to know now than to be sorry later. Some people think they know it all. A single aspect of love or maybe infatuation blinds them. Additionally, it is very difficult to find a good person these days. You know what I'm talking about, don't you?" she asked, and then continued, "I'm talking about a person who wants to give as well as share. A considerate person willing to accept someone for who they are. You understand what I'm trying to say?"

"Well, I'm not worried about other people. I am concerned about us. We want to be an inspiration to others. A forever relationship in which divorce is not an option."

Floretta sat still for a while. Several things went through her mind. She reflected on her past. It took her a few additional minutes to recollect her thought and share her life's story with Hope.

Floretta was very emotional. She had a sorrowful expression on her face. She took a couple of deep breaths. Hope sat attentively. She had never seen him look so eager to hear what she had to say. Hope maintained his composure. He did not want to make her more nervous. Eventually, she began to speak softly.

"Well, if my memory serves me right. No, let me rephrase that. I think I would like to start with my parents. My mom was a salesperson for a fashion design company. She was also a gifted tailor. She travelled a lot on her job. One day, after representing her company at a fashion show, she decided to fly back home that same evening. She had to change planes at the next major city. She was young and very attractive. Inclement weather delayed her flight. She was very concerned about that delay because her mother had just been released from the hospital after suffering a severe heart attack. In fact, she had been reluctant to attend the fashion show. However, that fashion show was a major event in her industry. They expected to make huge sales connections there, so she had to attend.

"As she waited for their flight to be announced, she saw someone staring at her in the waiting area. At first, she paid no attention. Suddenly, she had an urge to take a closer look at the person. To her surprise, she saw this good-looking man dressed in a navy blue three-piece suit. Their eyes met. He winked and smiled at her. She ignored him. A few seconds later, she felt him looking even more intensely at her. Their eyes met for the second time, and she saw him smiling at her. For some reason, she forgot all about her predicament and smiled back at him. He stood about six foot one inch tall, somewhat muscular.

"Mom became restless, got up from her seat, and took a stroll in the waiting area, to break up the boredom of her situation. She next pulled out her cell phone and called to check on her mother. Her call was not answered, which got her even more concerned and jittery. She wandered somehow in the direction of the man, who looked at her keenly. They struck up a conversation. She found out from their short conversation that he was on his way back home from a long-awaited vacation in the islands. He learned that she was in the fashion business, which accounted for the elegant attire she wore. At that point, their respective flights were announced on the public address system. They hurriedly exchanged phone numbers and parted company.

"When Mom arrived home, she found everything to be in order. A couple of weeks later, she gave him a call. They played phone tag for a while until they eventually connected. They were engaged in a long-distance relationship for several months. In the fullness of time, they sealed their relationship. They unsuccessfully tried to have children for over three years. Then at last they had a heartfelt conversation with themselves regarding the best option they might take."

Floretta's phone rang at that point. It was her mom, calling to remind her of their preplanned shopping trip to the mall. She and Hope agreed to continue this conversation some other time.

After Floretta left, Hope reviewed the employment package he received at CHIG. He perused all the documents he must complete to enroll in CHIG's scholarship program. The fact that CHIG would pay all his college-related expenses continued to excite him. He double-checked the grade requirements for continued sponsorship by CHIG. He wanted to make sure he informed Floretta correctly. He must maintain at least a B average. Upon successful graduation, he would be required to sign a five-year service contract with CHIG at the management level.

After careful consideration, he opted to complete the preliminary requirements for a degree program at Abokobi Community College (ACC) and then transfer to the prestigious TENA University, which had seven campuses with a total student enrollment of 49,000. Both were located in Giboad City.

Soon, a new workweek began. Hope had a chat with his supervisor, Ray, and Tina when he went to work on Monday. He expressed an interest in CHIG's sponsorship program for higher education.

Hope worked the morning shift from 7 a.m. to 3 p.m. Therefore, he could take his classes in the afternoon or evenings. That way, he could still have time to do his assignments and turn then in on time.

He took a coffee break at 10:30 a.m. Ray came into the break room around that same time. Therefore, Hope had the opportunity to discuss his educational plans with him in more detail. He told Ray that he would start taking face-to-face classes initially. However, he planned to switch to online classes after the second semester. Hopefully, he would have adjusted to full-time schedules at work and school.

Ray did not have any problems with that arrangement. He said he was willing to have someone cover Hope's shift if necessary. With that assurance, Hope turned in his scholarship paperwork to Tina's office during his lunch break.

"Good day, Ms. Doyer," he greeted Tina, who maintained an open-door policy.

"It is a beautiful day, isn't it?" she responded.

"Sure is. I'm happy to see you again."

"You are Hope, am I right? I remember that familiar face."

"Yes, Ms. Doyer, you have a great memory," he answered. "I am here to turn in my scholarship paperwork. I will be registering at ACC in the spring. I plan to take classes in the summer and fall so that I can get my associate's degree on a fast track and then transfer to TENA University shortly thereafter."

"No break in between schools, while working full-time? That is very ambitious! You will be a busy man, won't you? Have you decided on a major yet?"

"This is a great opportunity I cannot pass up. I have thought through it, and I think I can do my work and maintain my grades, as required. I know my work schedule and will have my course schedule as well. Therefore, I will fit in my study time into the free time. I will ensure that I have about five to six hours of sleep each night during the week. I have decided to major in Industrial Management with a minor in Environmental Science. I have already discussed that with my supervisor, Ray. He has no problems with it."

"Well, that leaves no room for entertainment or social activities for a young man like you, huh?" She continued, "I am very glad you have this opportunity. I have heard nothing but great things about you. They think you are very focused and serious-minded. You have also been asking many questions about our company. That is good. Of course, I had no doubts in my mind that you were the right candidate for your job."

"I do appreciate that. I will not let you down."

"I know you won't. It's that ingenious De Pinto blood. You have grown up looking more and more like Edmund, when he was alive. He would have been very proud of you."

"Yes, Ms. Doyer. I see him in my dreams every now and then. I know he is with me in the spirit. Life is not always fair," he said.

"We've all had our ups and down and disappointments. However, we must be thankful for what we have now. Edmund was a good man. A good-looking and hard-working family man, as I remember. I mean, as I heard. He touched the lives of many in a variety of ways. That means he cast his bread on the waters, and as is usually the case, he will find it after many days, maybe through you."

"I get the impression that you knew my dad personally. I miss him. Thanks for your kind words. They will resonate in my mind always. You are very kind, Ms. Doyer."

"There will be time for conversations about Avenice and old acquaintances," she said. "Well, young man, we will work on these papers for you as soon as possible. Keep up the good work. We are proud of you. Now, as you probably know by now, CHIG is continuing to grow. There will be other opportunities. I will let you know when everyone signs off on your scholarship papers, okay?"

"Thanks again, Ms. Doyer. I appreciate the opportunity." Hope had a sense of accomplishment as he left Tina's office. He completed his assignments for the day and soon it was time to go home.

He took an alternate route home from work that day. He stopped by a small city park to reflect some more about his day's accomplishments. From there he called to update Floretta about events. Certainly, they were elated by the manner in which matters progressed for the two of them.

On the Road to Success

It amazed Hope a good deal when he realized how fast time flew. His classes were scheduled to commence within a week of his registration at ACC. After a long spell of absence from formal classroom studies and homework assignments, he was a little nervous on his first day at school. He was, however, confident that he would adjust to the stress and strains of combining a normal course load with a forty-hour workweek.

Despite the numerous assignments from school, he made time to chat with Floretta each night before he went to bed. They spent most of the time together on weekends. Hope developed a favorable reputation with his professors and classmates.

He maintained an A average at school. He was determined to keep up his grades. He had a motto that guided him during his high school career, "To Be the Very Best or Among the Best."

One Saturday afternoon, an international bazaar was organized at ACC. That institution took pride in having the most diversified student population in Giboad City. A major objective of the bazaar was to portray the virtue of unity in diversity and the contributions of the various cultures to the advancement of humanity.

Students from the various countries represented on campus were invited to dress in their native attires. Several food stands were set up so that visitors could purchase and experience the taste of different foreign dishes. Additionally, there were cultural dances, poetry, and displays of arts and crafts. Aside from that, there were booths that displayed and provided information about native species of plants with medicinal values.

The event was a huge success because it attracted people from all occupations at Giboad City. Hope was among the attendees. At one of the booths, he struck up a conversation with a middle-aged, bespectacled man.

During the conversation that man discovered that Hope was a student at ACC. He asked about Hope's major. While Hope had a declared major and did well in his classes, the man detected a little bit of fuzzy logic in his response.

He formally introduced himself as Dr. Joseph Anderson, president of TENA University, and gave him his business card. He informed Hope that there would be an all-day aptitude test on their campus the following Saturday and that he should consider taking it. Later Hope should let him know how he did on that test. As they parted company, Hope noticed that Dr. Anderson wore a gold ring with a symbol of what looked like a glistening horseshoe on it.

Hope took him up on the suggestion; he registered for and took the aptitude test. When the results came in, Hope had scored 1341 out of a maximum total score of 1490. His strengths, according to the test results, were in the environmental sciences. That meant he had his declared major backward. He must switch his major from industrial management with a minor in environmental science to environmental science with a minor in industrial management when he transferred to TENA University.

Time has a way of working things out for those who catch it by its forelock. Slowly but surely, Hope followed his plan of action. In the course of time, he obtained his associate's degree from ACC. He discussed his circumstances with the counselor assigned to him at TENA University.

Ultimately, he contacted Dr. Anderson, whom he had met at the bazaar. He in turn put him in touch with the head of the environmental sciences department. Ultimately, that department confirmed his degree plan.

Hope maintained an A average at TENA University. He was consistently on the dean's list. Across the hallway from the dean's office was a large glass-encased bulletin board. It prominently displayed a list of the top ten students at the College of Arts and Sciences, together with their grades. Hope was on top of that list with a 4.0 GPA. His academically solid performance caught the eye of various interested parties at CHIG.

So powerful was the impact of Hope's academic performance at TENA University that it caused the authorities at CHIG to modify their scholarship program to allow him to pursue graduate studies at the university.

Upon his successful graduation, Hope received an upper-level management position. That happened at a time when the intensity of diversification and expansion of CHIG was high on its management's agenda.

CHIG's management scheduled a landmark meeting at its largest conference room. The chairman of the board, Elisha Zimmermann, was confirmed to attend. They included Hope among the list of participants. He was in upper management, very well educated and had displayed leadership skills. He was likable and analytical and by now had worked at CHIG for several years. Furthermore, he displayed interest in CHIG's expansion idea. He was also eloquent, bold, and persistent. Aside from that, the chairman of the board of CHIG had heard many good things about him, and wanted to check him out for himself.

Several presenters preceded Hope. He waited patiently for his turn. Tina formally introduced him as the next speaker. It was evident that he was well prepared for his presentation. Word was already out that he was an advocate. He boldly suggested Avenice as the prime location for CHIG's intended expansion.

He proposed several reasons to support that position. He argued that there CHIG would have ecosystem support for such a venture. He was a direct descendant of the founders of Avenice and consequently had viable connections to get the word out to the extended community there.

Additionally, Hope researched and conducted a cost analysis among other things for living, real estate, infrastructure, taxes, and transportation. He clearly demonstrated that CHIG's gains at Avenice would far outweigh their expenses and that there were promising business opportunities for CHIG at Avenice and its surrounding area.

Furthermore, he established a solid access of CHIG to a talent pool, with a large pool of skilled candidates with previous aerospace and military expertise and good consumer markets. Hope had taken into consideration the lifestyle and quality of life of the potential employee workforce at Avenice. He considered himself a core leader candidate for a startup operation. He also understood the community impacts and expectations.

During the recess at that meeting, Hope went to use the restroom. On his way out, he ran into Elisha Zimmermann. He gave Hope a firm handshake, pulled him to the side, and informed him he would recommend to the board that Hope lead a taskforce team to Avenice to ground-truth some of the points he had raised in his presentation pending a final decision. Oh! What a relief it was.

There again, after their handshake, Hope noticed that Elisha Zimmermann also wore a gold ring with the symbol of a glistening horseshoe, similar to that worn by Dr. Anderson, president of TENA University.

Marriage in the Air

Hope kept Floretta informed of developments at CHIG. Both she and her parents were elated by the turn of events for Hope. Floretta called to inform him she wanted to come over to his place the following morning.

When she walked in, Hope greeted her with the broadest smile on his face. She offered to prepare breakfast for both of them so that she could hear additional details from him firsthand and not over the phone.

"It was nice of you to prepare breakfast this morning. It has been a long time since you cooked something for me," said Hope.

"You are always too busy on Saturday mornings for me to do things like that for you. I imagine I can now do things like that for us more often."

"You are so sweet and understanding. I guess there are not many homey women like you around anymore. I am glad I found you."

"You really think so, or you now know so?" she asked.

"Do I have to answer that?"

"Of course you do. I love to hear you say things like that."

"You mean I score more points with you when I say rather than do things, huh?" he asked.

"Yep. By the way, I bought a brand-new bikini yesterday when I went shopping with Mom. It's very nice—nicer than the one I had on when we last went swimming. Mom picked it for me." She chuckled. "I guess like they say, Mama knows best."

"I can't wait to see it on you," he said.

"You will soon. I will try it on for you as soon as we finish breakfast. If you do not like it, then I won't wear it. I brought the other one with me just in case."

While Hope was still in the middle of eating breakfast, she stepped into the bathroom to put on the new bikini she bought the previous day. Hope was anxious to see how it fit on her.

Soon Floretta emerged and modeled her new bikini for Hope.

"My, my, my! That looks great on you. I like this one better than the other one."

"Guess how much it cost?" she asked.

"Oh, I bet it cost a fortune."

"As a matter of fact, it was much cheaper than the other one."

"Wow. It looks very, very expensive on you. I like the color on that million-dollar body of yours," he remarked.

They got ready for a date on the beach. It was a mild, calm day, with a gentle breeze and clear blue skies. Many people were at the beach. Some people played beach volleyball. Others flew kites. Most of those at the beach seemed to be there for a good swim, a good time, or both. Others brought colorful tents, lawn chairs and picnic tables, and some good home-cooked food for a family outing. There were also a few creative architectural facilities for beachside weddings.

Hope and Floretta spread a couple of large beach towels on the white sandy beach and watched the numerous activities around them. Every now and then they jumped into the calm, clear waters for a swim and then came back to lie down on their beach towels.

From their vantage point near one of the wedding stands, they clearly overheard the words of an official at a wedding going on only a few yards away. He was telling the marrying couple that marriage was God's idea and that it served as a building block of society. It was a commitment that led to oneness of the spirit, soul, and body. However, in a healthy marriage it was important for the marrying couple to understand and accept personality differences.

He went on to say that marriage replaced loneliness with companionship and completion. According to the fellow officiating that wedding, there were three prerequisites for a healthy marital relationship of commitment, completeness, and companionship. They were leaving, cleaving, and establishing a one-flesh relationship. The marrying couple must understand that their union required the forsaking of other relationships so that the husband and wife could be fully committed to each other.

He explained why marital vows were expressed in the presence of witnesses. It was to establish a permanent covenant in which the marrying couple acknowledged that they were inseparably united, completing one another physically, psychologically, and spiritually.

He cautioned that infidelity and divorce minimized the permanency and commitment thus established. Similarly, a lack of effective communication usually caused problems in a marriage. He mentioned three essential elements of effective communication, which included talking, listening, and caring.

Furthermore, a growing marriage is cultivated by years of mutual effort based upon trust of each other. In other words, a healthy marriage does not happen by chance processes alone. The marrying couple must work constantly at it.

Within a few minutes, the wedding ceremony was over. Hope looked Floretta in the eye, and then said, "I love you, babe."

"I love you too," she promptly replied.

"You are such a wonderful woman to me. I feel complete whenever you are around me."

"I feel the same way about you."

"I know you do," he said. "You have told me that before. I believe you are sincere in what you tell me, always. You have been patient with school activities, my work schedule, and me. You never complained about us not being together for entire weeks. You bought into my schedule and are very understanding of my situation. If you did not love or care for me, you wouldn't be staying alone at home all this time waiting for the days of the week to go by so that we can be together on the weekend. You have invested all your time in me. You have given me the love and care that I need. What more can a man ask for?"

"Well, if you love a person, you make many sacrifices to show him that you care. I understand that you have to work, study, and all that. Don't get me wrong. I do get lonely sometimes," she said.

"I don't want you to be lonely. You make me feel sad when you say things like that. Let me say again that I do feel on top of the world when you assure me of your love for me. There is so much the two of us can accomplish together."

"I know that, Hope. There is much more love and happiness I want to give you, darling. You are my first love. My true love. I will not share you with anyone."

"You have nothing to worry about," he assured her. "If there's anyone on earth I must share my life with, it will be you."

"Are you sure of that?"

"Of course I am. I am tired of coming home from work each day to an empty apartment. I always feel the need for you to be by my side, so that I can share my ideas with you. I now understand much better why a companion was made for Adam, in the garden. Truly, it is not good for a man to be alone."

"I know it is hard for you to go through all that," she said. "I sometimes wonder how you do that. By the way, do you realize the seriousness of the reference you just made, Hope?"

"I meant everything I have told you. I don't play with matters like that."

"It is good to know where I stand with you. How can you fit me into your full-time work schedule, special projects you have undertaken at work, and all that?"

"When there's a will, there must be a way. You wanted that flower vase very badly, and you got it. Did that teach you something?" he asked.

"We will talk about that later, not now. There was a lot more to that than meets the eye," she said with a giggle.

"Really?"

"Really!" she said. "I bet Mom would have a fit to hear about something like that. She'd be glad to see me get married someday. However, she's used to having me around the house for so long that the idea of me leaving home would tear her to pieces."

"Are you going to give her a hint, periodically?"

He went on to ask her what she thought an ideal husband could do to improve on a marital relationship. She stated that an ideal husband, in her opinion, should find creative ways to do special things for his wife, regularly share his hopes and plans, and listen to those of his wife.

She paused for a moment. Then she added that the husband should be sensitive to his wife's emotional needs. Additionally, he must tune in to her feelings. Equally important, the husband must look for his spouse's strengths and praise her for them; he should not get slack on courtesy and good manners and must avoid a domineering and bossy attitude. He must do his very best to learn new things about her, especially things she enjoyed; he must not compare his wife to other women. He must encourage her in her activities and by all means keep himself spiritually, mentally and physically fit.

Next, Floretta asked Hope what he thought an ideal wife should do to strengthen their marriage. He at first smiled and then carefully responded that the wife should in turn find creative ways to do special things for her husband; look for his strengths, and praise him for them genuinely. She should strive to learn new things about him, especially those that he enjoyed; should not compare him to other men; should encourage him in his activities; and finally continually strive to be spiritually, mentally, and physically fit.

They next discussed what couples should strive to do in order to keep their marriage strong. At that point, Hope reached out for a pen and small notepad he had in the picnic bag. He made notes of what they discussed.

He wrote down the following things: Do not nag or taunt each other. Do financial planning together. Do a good job at reaching a unified attitude on credit, spending, and savings. Never go to bed with unresolved anger or grievances. Practice the art of effective communication. Resolve to make the best of what is rather than fantasizing about what might have been. Notice each other, especially when in public, and never make a public remark at the expense of your mate. Look for common activities and interests and try to develop them. Plan a weekend retreat or vacation alone with your mate at least once a year.

"It would be better to give such hints to my dad instead. She might never get over it," she replied.

"When the right time comes, I will man up and give it to both of them straight. That will be the day, won't it?"

"Mom will have lots of questions for you."

"Well, so much for that. I guess we should be getting back to the apartment," suggested Hope.

"Whatever you want to do is fine with me. Come on, let's get going."

Floretta returned home very late that evening, having spent the entire day with the man of her dreams. She was a happy woman, especially after the interesting, serious conversations with Hope.

As she walked into their house, her mother looked at her intensely with her eyebrows raised. Her instincts probably told her that a significant turn of events was about to take place.

The relationship between Hope and Floretta continued to grow. They talked to each other more and more frequently. Floretta went out with him more often over the weekends. Hope also visited her frequently at home, even if only for a few minutes.

Irene sensed how close and attached her daughter was to Hope and continued to ask many questions about him. Those frequent conversations gave Floretta a chance to present Hope in a much more favorable and responsible light to her mother.

Soon, it was obvious that the bond of friendship between Hope and Floretta was impregnable from any outside sources. One afternoon, as she helped her mother in the kitchen, mother and daughter got into another lengthy conversation. Initially, it centered on life in general. However, it slowly evolved subtly around her serious relationship with Hope.

Floretta did not hide anything from her mother regarding their strong relationship. She made it clear from her responses that she was head over heels in love with him. Even though she did not say it openly, her mother got the impression that a permanent relationship was imminent. Then Irene changed the subject, as if she desired to allow the startling things she heard from Floretta to sink in.

Shortly thereafter, Barry came home from work. He could immediately sense that his wife's mood was different. They had dinner and retired to the den to watch TV. A two-hour special program featured Floretta's favorite artists, keeping her virtually glued to the TV set. That gave her mom the opportunity to ask Barry to take her to the convenience store to get a couple of items she'd forgotten to get earlier in the day.

On their way to the store, she recounted in detail her talk with Floretta regarding Hope. All along, Barry thought highly of Hope. He considered him an ambitious young man who was goal-oriented. Although she also liked Hope, it was obvious to Barry that his wife was jittery about the real possibility that Floretta could leave home soon. She knew that eventually that time would come. However, she was unprepared for it.

"What makes you so sure that Floretta will be leaving home soon?" Barry asked.

"I suggest you talk to your daughter candidly," she responded. "She is absolutely consumed with feelings and thoughts about him. I am a woman, and I know that no woman would ever talk like that about a man unless she has marriage to him on her mind."

"You said the right word. She is a woman. She is no longer a child. In our many talks, Hope has not mentioned anything to me about his ultimate intentions about Floretta. I don't believe either of them would hide something that important from us."

"Well, that was all I wanted to share with you. I was nervous about sharing that with you in her presence," she cautioned. "That was why we had to leave the house. Do not get me wrong. I like him. He is a nice young man, but he is not from Giboad City. I am concerned that if they should get married, he might take her back to his hometown, and all the fruit of our labor will be in vain. Since you do not see things the way I do, I guess I will have to wait and see how this saga ends. Let me get a carton of eggs, before we get back to the house. Please, Barry, don't say anything to her about my concerns."

While her parents were out of the house, Floretta received a call from one of her friends next door during a commercial break. She wanted to know how she had enjoyed that special show on TV.

When her parents walked into the house and saw her on the phone, her mom immediately assumed she was on the phone with Hope. She looked at her husband and winked, as if to say, *I told you, she never can go for a night without calling him.* However, she was wrong in her suspicion.

Nothing significantly different happened for the following few weeks. In his own subtle ways, Barry tried to assuage his wife's fears regarding Floretta and Hope's imminent union as husband and wife. Most people in the neighborhood felt the impact of Hope and Floretta's relationship.

Occasionally, a next-door neighbor tried to poke her nose into their business by asking when Hope and Floretta were going to cut the wedding cake. They all thought he would make Floretta a good husband.

Under siege from the continued gossip in the neighborhood, Irene felt the pressure to do something about the situation. She was the type of woman who liked to maintain a clean image of herself and her family as pious and old-fashioned, a self-righteous woman who took it upon herself to counsel others on moral issues.

She was concerned that people might be saying behind her back, "Physician, heal thyself," because the once-reclusive Floretta spent almost all her weekends with a man she was not married to. As time went by, Irene came to grips with the inevitable reality.

Soon it was time for Christmas. Hope asked Floretta what might be an appropriate gift from him for her parents. She suggested that anything nice that could be displayed on the large entertainment center in their family room might be appropriate. She then asked him what he was going to get her for Christmas. Hope assured her that he would let her know by that weekend.

Floretta waited patiently for that weekend. She called him promptly on Saturday morning to find out what he got her for Christmas. Obviously, Hope could sense a certain amount of anxiety in her voice.

"Hello, honey. What's up?" she asked

"Not a thing. How are things going at your end?"

"A little bit of everything. Have you made up your mind yet, or should I keep wondering?"

"What are you talking about?" he asked in return.

"Didn't you tell me you were going to let me know what you are will get me for Christmas today?"

"Yes, I did. But the day is still young."

"You mean you don't have an idea? I'm just curious," she said.

"I can't say it on the phone."

"Why can't you?"

"Because it is something I must tell you personally," he replied.

"Are you saying you will be coming over here today?"

"Yes, around three p.m. Is that all right?"

"I can't wait until three. I'd like to know now," she said.

"All right, I'll be there as soon as I get through cleaning my apartment. Will your parents be home, as well?"

"As far as I know. See you soon. I love you, babe."

Floretta paced up and down in the den. Her parents detected she was uneasy about something after she got off the phone with Hope. She could not sit still. Each time she heard the sound of a car stop in front of their house, she drew the curtain apart and looked out to see if it was Hope.

Eventually he showed up. She hugged and kissed him on the cheek as he entered the house. She never did that in the presence of her parents. She could no longer hide her feelings for Hope even in their presence. She sat down close to Hope and held his hands.

Hope felt Floretta's body almost trembling, as she got closer and closer to him on the love seat. "What's the matter with you today?" he asked.

"You have kept me in so much suspense about my Christmas present. Hurry and tell me, my darling."

"I have decided to get you a ring, an engagement ring," he said confidently.

"A ring—for real?" she asked.

"Yes, and I came to pick you up and take you to the jewelry store so that you can select the design yourself. I picked two I know you would like because I know your taste. But in situations like this, I think two heads will be better than one."

"A ring. An engagement ring. Oh my God!" she exclaimed.

Her parents were in the family room at that time. Her mom's itchy ears did not allow her to sit still either. As soon as she heard Floretta mention a ring, she rushed to the den to investigate what was going on.

"Barry, come in here. Did someone make mention of a ring?" she asked.

Floretta stared at Hope for a second. She then asked him to respond to her mother's question. At that point, Hope got on one knee and pulled a hundred-dollar bill from his back pocket. He wrapped it around Floretta's ring finger and asked her if she would agree to marry him until he placed the real ring on her finger. She immediately said, "*Yes*, I will."

"That sounds great to me," said Barry.

"Is that all you are going to say, honey?" Irene asked her husband.

"Have you two discussed this in advance?" asked Barry. "Are you sure you love each other strongly enough to share your lives together?"

"Yes, we do, and we have talked extensively about it. We love and understand each other. We can no longer stay apart," responded Hope.

"Unless your mom has anything else to say, you two have our blessings to get married," added Barry.

"Floretta is the apple of my eye," Irene said. "Barry, can we step out into our bedroom for a minute?"

Both Floretta and Hope were tense for a while, as her parents excused themselves to their bedroom. They would not know what to do if an unexpected glitch developed. After some twenty minutes in the privacy of their bedroom, her parents came out with more seriousness than they ever displayed.

Floretta's mother was the first to speak. "After very careful consideration of what the two of you have decided to do, we have decided that … Well, Barry, why don't you tell them what we decided?" she said to her husband.

At that point, Floretta trembled. However, Hope stood still, confident that they would hear the right decision from both of her parents.

"Stop trembling, dear," Barry said. "There is no need to. Smile, you two have both of our blessings to get married. What date did you have in mind?"

Upon hearing that favorable decision, Hope embraced Floretta. He expressed his utmost appreciation to her parents for the confidence they had in him, as well as their faith in him as her soul mate.

Floretta turned around to look at her mother. She walked toward her and embraced her. Mother and daughter shed tears of joy on their shoulders. Floretta wiped the tears from her face and then from her mother's. She stepped back and stood beside Hope. That was a gesture to her parents that he would be her husband on Christmas Day.

Preparations for the wedding began right away. It took a lot of organization and coordination to make that day as remarkable and exceptionally memorable as could possibly be. All the preparations went well, as expected. Wedding invitations were printed and sent out weeks in advance.

Both Hope and Floretta received calls from well-wishers and friends. The news caught on like wildfire at CHIG. From all indications, everyone expected it to be a very expensive ceremony indeed.

Floretta chose Beula and Estella as bridesmaids. Most of the neighbors considered them instrumental in Hope and Floretta's relationship. Had they not invited her to that carnival, Floretta might not have met Hope.

As it turned out, nearly 490 guests attended the wedding ceremony. It really was very colorful and creative. The reception after the wedding was exceptionally interesting. The rose garden behind the chapel was the venue.

The rosebushes in the garden followed specific patterns of arrangement. Each row had a different variety of rosebush. Caretakers meticulously trimmed the hedges around the garden. Similarly, they mowed the lawns around the compound regularly.

Food was served buffet style. There was plenty to eat and drink. Photographers at the wedding made a fortune that day. Gift upon gift was the order of that day. The ceremony ended with a special well-wishing and goodwill speech by the parents of the bride.

Hope and Floretta spent their wedding night together for the first time as man and wife at Bev's Inn and Resort. It was one of the most expensive inns of its kind in town.

Their matrimonial dreams had finally come true. All the nervous feelings they had the previous day went away. It took Hope a while to get used to referring to Floretta as Mrs. De Pinto. That was a title his mother, Charlotte, had for many years. Every time he referred to Floretta as such, it brought back memories of the good old days in Avenice when the De Pinto family unit was intact.

It all sounded like a dream to him. He and his wife had to adjust to family life. They discussed a destination for their honeymoon. However, urgent plans for business development and expansion at CHIG for which Hope was an integral catalyst, caused them to postpone their plans for a honeymoon.

15

Preparations for Revival of the "Sankofa" Dream

By all business yardsticks of measurement, CHIG had established itself as a leader in the industrial marketplace. However, CHIG's ambitious leadership was not complacent. They continually aspired to venture into greater business opportunities.

Hope took stock of himself and the progress he made thus far. He continued to read voraciously. He drew inspiration from a mythical figure called Joseph who incidentally was destined for success. Nevertheless, his siblings were jealous of his perceived destiny. They threw him into a pit of destruction to derail him from his destiny.

However, as often happens, the forces of good mysteriously outwitted those of evil. Ultimately, with patience and in due time, the forces of good operated supernaturally behind the scenes to rescue Joseph from that pit. He got free transportation to a place where the greatness embedded in him unfolded.

That story played back in his mind repeatedly. As such, through it all, he never faltered or lost hope of rising above the trials he faced. He was determined not to fall victim to the storms of life. He would not allow them to throw him into the pit of sadness and despair. If that happened, his hope to rescue Avenice from economic decline would vanish. Additionally, the dream of his parents for him to redeem their family name and honor, or develop a profession for himself and thus make life more meaningful and purposeful, would also vanish.

Thus, even though Hope had a strong will to keep his head above water, he continually sank into deep, pensive meditative states. He disciplined himself to seek spiritual guidance on grounds of faith. He needed divine intervention for his ultimate success.

He needed strength and encouragement in various dimensions of his well-being. For example, it took mental strength and self-discipline to be alone with his God. He constantly desired to experience God's presence and hear His voice. Consequently, during his times of weakness, he fell on his face and prayed in his sanctum so that he could experience the intercessory work of God.

One spiritual secret that came out of his meditations was an emphasis on the need for him to continue to eradicate remnants of negative emotions. The spiritual awareness of that was very vivid. He knew that negative emotions are anathema to our spiritual well-being. They cause the unenlightened to live in fear. Hope had the spiritual awareness as never before that when people allow fear to overwhelm them, they are unable to see or think through the unexpected storms of life. Suddenly, the trials they face seem bigger to them than the limitless power of the almighty God. Consequently, they tend to lose focus on God as the object of their faith. Wavering faith or doubt in the ability of God are obstacles to answered prayer because they throw the afflicted into a state of helplessness and hopelessness.

In keeping with the directive of Elisha Zimmermann, Hope formed a committee at CHIG to address in detail the reasons to select Avenice as a primary choice for CHIG's business ventures. Among other things, he charged them with the specific tasks of working with him to address the following in their report to CHIG's board of directors:

1. Perform an analysis of the cost of living encompassing real estate, infrastructure, transportation, and taxes. The bottom line was that in order to be profitable, the projected income gains of CHIG must outweigh the increase in CHIG's expenditure in that business proposition.
2. Establish the existence of proximity to target consumer market.
3. Can CHIG get access to a larger talent pool?
4. Provide evidence that demonstrates a thorough understanding of the demographics of Avenice, including an evaluation of the actual need relative to the desire to expand.
5. Lifestyle/quality of life in Avenice
6. Core leader candidates, i.e., Hope's ability to identify and send candidates from CHIG to ensure that Avenice fits into CHIG's company culture.
7. Community impacts.
8. Ecosystem Support. That is to say, does CHIG have or know anyone with the right connections to make its objectives happen in Avenice?

The team members had regular planning meetings. They surfed the internet to obtain relevant information and made phone and email contacts with organizations they thought might be helpful for their objectives. Nevertheless, they wanted to have a couple of days in advance to tour Avenice before formal business meetings and other activities began. That was not applicable to Hope, though, since he was a native of Avenice. Hope and his team flew to Avenice the following Friday evening. They checked into a five-star hotel for the entire week.

The following morning, a minivan took them on a tour of the city. Hope knew all along the exact spot he had in mind for the location of CHIG's potentially new plant. He had a vivid recollection of that specific location. He saw it in one of his dreams.

The site looked exactly as he previously saw in his dream. The branches of the huge oak tree that stood in front of a partially completed chapel swayed from side to side, as if it welcomed their presence. That site was close to but not technically within the western boundary of Avenice.

He was also aware of a conservation easement his ancestors, the founders of Avenice, had in place that prohibited improvements of that part of the city in perpetuity. When they got to that specific location, there was a unanimous consensus that the site was ideal for the location of CHIG's new plant, if approved.

They returned to their hotel to talk things over early that evening. Hope rented a car that evening. He was curious to visit the neighborhood where he grew up. Privately, he wanted to find out about the status of his mother and Jimmy. He was of course aware that the place where Charlotte and Jimmy worked had gone bankrupt and closed down.

Though he had been away from Avenice for several years, he still remembered his way around town. Of course, with the existence of Global Positioning System (GPS) equipment in cars and cell phone, he could navigate the city to any place he wanted to go.

Traffic had subsided at the time he left the hotel. Thus, within forty-five minutes he made it close to the neighborhood where he grew up. He passed by the YMCA where he had briefly worked several years ago.

It was almost dark by the time he got to the neighborhood where he grew up. The tinted windows of his car prevented any interested or familiar faces from seeing him clearly.

He drove across the railroad tracks where he'd caught a ride on a train when he left Avenice, and within a few short minutes, he arrived close to Charlotte's address. He pulled to the side of the road to gather his thoughts.

The events that took place prior to and on the day he left home flashed on his mind. He could not hold back the tears that ran down his cheeks. They progressively became heavier and heavier. He felt them as tears of blood. The front porch light was on, but there were no vehicles in the driveway.

He sat still in his car for several minutes. Then, out of the clear blue sky, he saw a car in his rearview mirror with a turn signal that indicated the driver's intention to pull into Charlotte's driveway. A woman got out first and got a wheelchair from the trunk of the car.

She pushed the wheelchair to the passenger side of the car and opened the door for the passenger. The woman was his mother, Charlotte. The man in the wheelchair was Jimmy.

Hope's emotions got the better part of him. He sat in his rented car and wept bitterly. For a moment, he considered getting out of his car to reveal himself to his mother and Jimmy. However, a still small voice within himself cautioned that it was not yet time to do so.

From that vantage point, he watched his mother help Jimmy into the wheelchair. She wheeled him inside the house and then returned to close the car doors and lock the front door to her house. Hope left the scene and drove back to his hotel room to recuperate from the powerful emotional experience.

Next morning, the tour minivan took them to other scenic parts of Avenice. Throughout the economic downturn, the city government had done all it could to maintain the scenic beauty of Avenice. They implemented a variety of attractive economic packages to attract potential investors to the city.

The group that traveled with Hope retired to bed early that evening since they had scheduled several business meetings for the rest of the week. Hope, however, continued to be curious about his mother and Jimmy. Therefore, he planned a second trip to his childhood neighborhood. He drove by the two high schools he had attended and the YMCA, where he had briefly worked.

He also drove by the house where his late friend and confidant, Roger, lived. Those brief stopovers brought back memories of how far he had come from the time he left Avenice to an unknown destination that ultimately led him to Giboad City.

After he got to his boyhood home, he noticed that the backyard garden his late father, Edmund, had kept was no longer there. Their entire house was dilapidated and needed a lot of restoration. The beautiful flowers and vibrant grass lawn that once adorned their front yard were overgrown with noxious weeds. Even they seemed neglected, watered only by seasonal rainfall.

Shortly, darkness replaced the twilight of sunset. He saw no signs of the presence of either Charlotte or Jimmy in the house. The front porch light had been left on. Hope waited in vain for a few more minutes in anticipation for the arrival of Charlotte or Jimmy home.

Consequently, he drove back to his hotel in despair. Due to the numerous stopovers he made, Hope was running low on gas. Consequently, he stopped at a convenience store to gas up before he returned to his hotel.

He filled up his gas tank at a nearby convenience store. While in the process of replacing the gas tank cap, Hope heard a familiar laugh from a woman who came out of the convenience store. Due to poor lighting at that place, he could not get a good glimpse of her. That familiar laugh reminded him of Beverly.

Still, he was unsure of that assumption. The bespectacled woman he saw from the distance was a little heavier. She also wore her hair a little shorter than the Beverly he remembered as a young man in that neighborhood. Be that as it might, Hope got into his car and drove off to his hotel.

Hope and his team had scheduled a meeting with a reputable environmental consulting company the next morning. He reviewed the topographic maps he had of the site that he thought was ideal for CHIG's new plant if approved. As an environmental scientist, he made a notation in his notepad to request a comprehensive Environmental Impact Statement of the site and the adjacent area.

They had a very busy, productive week with all the professional staff of the consulting company they were working with on the investigative elements of the task that brought them to Avenice.

The consulting company was a reputable multidisciplinary professional services firm. They served as consultants for some of the more progressive aeronautics companies in Avenice during its heyday. Therefore, they had intimate knowledge about Avenice and the surrounding areas.

After completing the first leg of their investigative work, Hope and his team returned to Giboad City with high hopes that they were probably on the right track of something very favorable with regard to Hope's vision for Avenice.

The Gathering of Dark Clouds

Hope exuded a noticeable vibrant energy upon his return to Giboad City. It was so strong that people close to him could feel there was something clearly different about him.

He shared their experiences with his wife, Floretta, who was eager to know what they had accomplished on that trip. In the quietness of their living room, she struck up a conversation about his trip with her husband.

"How was your trip, darling?" she inquired.

"We accomplished a lot, much more than I expected."

"I figured that you did. I can observe your confidence level is through the roof, so to speak."

"Really?" he asked.

"Yes, that's right. Your visage and attitude tell it all."

"I am glad we went to Avenice to ground-truth my convictions for it to be a prime location for CHIG's new ventures. The consulting company we met with had a very knowledgeable, experienced professional staff.

"We had a very productive meeting. All the members of our team agreed with the site I identified for the proposed expansion. Everything fell in place like clockwork."

"Tell me more," she said.

"Aside from that I took a private trip to various sites of interest."

"Really? And might those include your childhood neighborhood?"

"You are very intuitive," he responded.

"Of course I am. I married you, didn't I?"

"You are right about that. I drove by the high schools I attended and ultimately to my childhood neighborhood. This GPS equipment comes in handy, especially for those of us who hate to stop and ask for directions, if you know what I mean."

"You are right about that. Did you get to see your family house, and your mom?" she asked.

"I parked at a vantage point near our family house. I did not think it was the right time to reestablish broken relationships. It has been quite a long time since my departure from home. However, I did see my mom and her friend, Jimmy, from a distance. Jimmy was in a wheelchair, and the house was dilapidated." He paused, and tears ran down his cheeks.

"Well, now that things are beginning to happen at CHIG, I guess you might have to take additional trips to Avenice, and maybe I can come along with you and meet your mom one of these days," she said.

"Yes, I hope so too. I hope that time comes soon."

"You remember the conversation we started a while back when you asked me about my family?" she asked. "We did not finish that conversation. I think now is the time to continue that conversation, don't you think so?"

"Certainly. Things developed rapidly between us, and we did not get the chance to discuss many things. I agree that we should," he responded.

"I think we were at the point where I informed you about my mom's difficulties with conception. Ultimately, she and Barry decided to adopt a baby. I was that baby. So now, you know I am an adopted child. Does that make any difference to you?"

"Of course not. When I told you I loved you, I really meant that. Certainly, our children may want to know about their ancestry. Similarly, it is good to be aware of things in our DNA for various reasons, but we will not worry about that yet," he responded.

"I requested a comprehensive Environmental Impact Study for the site I had in mind for CHIG's possible expansion site," he continued. "I cannot wait to get the full report, study it, and then give a presentation to Elisha Zimmermann and CHIG's board. I believe that I am on the right track. I do not have any doubts about the way I feel about my proposal. That is why I do not seem nervous. That is the new attitude you see in me, my darling."

At that point of their conversation, Hope got a call from Tina Doyer. She informed him that Elisha had been rushed to the hospital. She intended to give him a follow-up call later that day.

Hope asked the nature of Elisha's medical problem. Tina explained that in his youthful years, Elisha Zimmermann had worked for several years at a petrochemical plant that produced the chemicals benzene and toluene. Lately, he had complained about headaches, fatigue, and shortness of breath. Furthermore, he was easily bruised and had tiny red spots under his skin. He had lost weight steadily for no apparent reason. He complained about night sweats, intermittent fever, and itching.

Results of several laboratory tests ordered by his primary care physician, and medical specialists confirmed that he had myeloproliferative neoplasm.

Since he did not respond to a plethora of established drug treatments, his healthcare providers evaluated his situation and opted for an allogeneic stem cell transplant procedure. That required removal of tissue from family members or donors. The cells thus obtained would be injected into Elisha after he had undergone chemotherapy.

Tina wondered if Hope might agree to be part of the screening process, should they be unable to match a donor from his family. Hope immediately agreed. He was willing to do whatever it took to save the life of Elisha at that critical stage of business development decisions at CHIG.

Elisha Zimmermann was not only the chairman of the board for CHIG. He was also Hope's ardent supporter. Therefore, it would be highly devastating to lose him at that critical period of CHIG's expansion process.

Thus, screening of Elisha's known family members began. Since time was of the essence, anxious moments set in. For a while, it seemed that none of the tissue obtained from Elisha's family or the donor registry matched his.

Elisha's situation was grim and desperate. Dr. Anderson volunteered to be screened as a potential donor. However, his tissue type did not match that of Elisha. Seven days into the search for a suitable donor, Hope checked in as a potential donor.

He had been to the same hospital on numerous occasions due to complications associated with Floretta's pregnancy. They removed tissues from his pelvis for analysis to determine if his human leukocyte antigen (HLA) proteins closely matched Elisha's.

To everyone's relief and excitement, his test results confirmed that his HLA proteins closely matched those of Elisha. Consequently, they used Hope's tissues to perform the stem cell transplant procedure. It was very successful because Elisha did not have any side effects such as graft-versus-host disease, increased risk of bleeding, anemia, fatigue, or mouth sores.

A Desire for Reunion

Amid all those developments, Hope had his hands full. Floretta went into true labor. He rushed her to the same hospital where Elisha was admitted. He had never missed a day of work since he became a full-time employee at CHIG. However, circumstances beyond his control required him to attend to the medical needs of both Elisha and his wife.

Because of the position of the fetus and other issues with the placenta, her gynecologist/obstetrician opted to perform a cesarean section to deliver the baby.

In preparation for her delivery, Floretta was taken to the delivery room. The nurses who attending to her followed that hospital's standard operating procedures. For example, after she was undressed and covered with a hospital gown, Floretta was positioned on an operating table. They put in a urinary catheter prior to wheeling her to the operating room.

Furthermore, they inserted an intravenous (IV) line in her arm. For safety reasons, the nurses strapped her legs to hold her on the table. The hair around the surgical site was neatly shaved, and her skin was cleaned with an antiseptic solution.

Floretta's abdomen was draped with sterile material. A drape was also placed above her chest to screen the surgical site. A spinal block would be applied by her anesthesiologist to numb the abdomen to her legs and feet. Her anesthesiologist continuously watched her heart rate, blood pressure, breathing, and blood oxygen level during the procedure.

They explained to her that once the anesthesia took effect, it was anticipated that her obstetrician would make a transverse incision above her pubic bone. They cautioned her about hearing the sounds of an electrocautery machine, which would seal off bleeding.

Subsequently deeper incisions would be made through the tissues and separate the muscles until the uterine wall was reached. Finally, an additional horizontal incision would be made in the uterus.

At that point, her obstetrician would open the amniotic sac and deliver the baby through the opening. Floretta was again cautioned she might feel some pressure or a pulling sensation. The umbilical cord would be cut, after which she would get medicine in her IV to help the uterus contract and expel the placenta.

However, that was not all. The obstetrician would carefully remove the placenta and examine the uterus for tears or pieces of placenta. Then sutures would close the incision in the uterine muscle and reposition the uterus in the pelvic cavity.

After that, the muscle and tissue layers as well as the skin incision would be closed with sutures or surgical staples. Then finally, a sterile bandage would be applied. "In the recovery room, nurses will watch your blood pressure, breathing, pulse, bleeding, and the firmness of your uterus," he told her.

Both Floretta and Hope were further told that they could be with their baby while in the recovery area, after the newborn baby had been monitored in the nursery for a short time. Floretta could then start breastfeeding in the recovery area.

"After an hour or two in the recovery area, you will be moved to your hospital room for the rest of your hospital stay." Since that was their first baby, and in light of the fact that Floretta's mom had never experienced childbirth, her attending physician gave her additional detailed instructions.

He informed her that as the anesthesia wore off, she might get pain medicine as needed from the attending nurses or through a device connected to her IV line called a patient-controlled analgesia or PCA pump. In some cases, pain medicine might be given through the epidural catheter until it was removed.

The physician further informed Floretta that she might have gas pains as the intestinal tract started working again after surgery. She was encouraged to get out of bed, since moving around and walking would help ease gas pains.

She might also receive prescription pain medicine to take at home. It was likely Floretta could experience uterine contractions, called after-pains, for a few days. The uterus would continue to contract over several weeks.

The urinary catheter would be removed the day after surgery. She might be given liquids to drink a few hours after surgery. Gradually, she could eat more solid foods as she could can handle them.

Finally, she might be given antibiotics in her IV while in the hospital and a prescription to keep taking the antibiotics at home. She was given her discharge instructions and asked to arrange a follow-up visit with her gynecologist two to three weeks after the surgery.

Hope and Floretta had a healthy baby despite the previous challenges of her pregnancy. They went through the usual routine of changing diapers and learning their baby's body language. Hope helped Floretta with the additional responsibilities that came with the newborn child at home in addition to executing his forty-hour workweek at CHIG.

Their baby had both of their bodily characteristics. In fact, he inherited the birthmark on Floretta's eyelid. However, as time went by he took on more of the characteristics of his grandfather, Edmund. It was proper that they named him Edmund II.

With the arrival of Edmund II, the Pritchards suggested that they moved back home with them pending the outcome of the business developments at CHIG. However, Hope wanted to be his own man. Therefore, he temporarily relocated his family into a two-bedroom apartment.

From his suitcase, Hope retrieved and reframed the picture of his father that fell and broke in their living room when Jimmy went into a furious rage. He had brought it with him when he left home in Avenice but kept it concealed until their baby was delivered. He hung it on the wall of their baby's room. Before long the baby crawled and then learned how to walk.

Meanwhile, Elisha continued to recover from his health issues. So remarkable was his recovery that he resumed his normal workload. Everyone was appreciative of what Hope had done to safe Elisha's life, as well as the renewed vision and mission for CHIG.

Rumors circulated whether there could be a possible blood relationship between him and Hope. Nevertheless, no one bothered to conduct an ancestral search to verify that. One observation that was obvious was that Dr. Anderson paid more frequent visits to Elisha than previously. Nevertheless, whatever they discussed was strictly kept behind closed doors. No one was privy to it.

Finally, the comprehensive Environmental Impact Statement report Hope requested was finalized and delivered to him. There were several anxious moments as he read that report. The report was very thorough and detailed. It corroborated all the points Hope presented in his justification of Avenice as the primary site for CHIG's expansion ventures. However, there was more.

As a qualified environmental scientist, Hope read the report repeatedly. A section of the report caught his attention. He then read slowly and reviewed the exhibits that came along with it.

After Hope reviewed the report, he came across certain data that raised his level of curiosity about the possible existence of minerals in the western fringes of Avenice.

He therefore requested a follow up investigative study using the most current technologies in mineral exploration. He specifically requested data Landsat images, indexed calculations of certain minerals, and a color composite and band ratio of different spectral bands.

The consulting company subcontracted the work to a reputable company that used equipment fitted with hyperspectral sensors to collect spectral data from aircraft that used infrared, near infrared, and shortwave technology. Such data could provide information on the spatial distribution of gold deposits in the study area.

Furthermore, Hope ordered and received certified copies of the original modified conservation easements his grandfather, B.T., had put in place to protect the western fringes of Avenice.

No matter the instruments and safeguards put in place to prevent leakage of CHIG's investigative efforts in Avenice, it appeared that there was always a fly on the wall of guarded places. As such, some of that information leaked among certain segments of the population in Avenice.

They knew for example that there was a real possibility that a native son of Avenice had a real chance of relocating a major plant in town. However, due to the failure of previous businesses that had relocated to Avenice, not many paid much attention to that rumor.

At about this time, Jimmy's health issues had compounded. He was at a long-term care facility that left Charlotte all alone at home. She longed for her son. She had time to evaluate the circumstances that had led to the severance of the solid relationship she had with her son and the possible contributions of Jimmy to that broken relationship. For all those years that Hope was gone from Avenice, Charlotte never changed her phone number.

Several years had gone by without any contact between them. In fact, she did not know whether Hope was dead or alive. She directed all her attention to satisfying Jimmy. She had not caught on to Jimmy's schemes that frustrated Hope to the point of his running away from home. She recalled Hope's fruitless efforts to get an audience with her to discuss his inner feelings.

She also remembered the dreams she and Edmund had for their only son—that he would be the heir from the De Pinto family to restore their family prestige and revive the economic standing of Avenice, hopefully better than it used to be.

After their follow-up study of the western fringes of Avenice, the consulting company invited Hope for a meeting once again at the study area in Avenice. It was not necessary for the entire team to be at the site. They just wanted Hope there.

Hope discussed this with his wife. They agreed that Floretta and Edmund II would accompany him to that meeting. Floretta could tell from his body language that he longed for a reunion with his mother.

They arrived on a Friday night and stayed at the same hotel where Hope and his team stayed previously. The following Saturday morning Hope dialed his mother's number. The phone continued to ring unanswered. He kept trying until after the third attempt Charlotte answered her phone.

"Hello," she said.

"Hello, is this the De Pinto residence?" he asked.

"Yes, it is. May I know who is calling?" she asked. Charlotte thought something had happened to Jimmy at the long-term care facility. As it happened, Beverly had stopped by to check on her and was still there.

"Mom, this is Hope, your son," he replied.

Charlotte accidentally dropped the phone in shock. Beverly hugged her as a source of encouragement. She was anxious to know details of the phone call.

"What happened? Who called? Is Jimmy okay?" inquired Beverly.

Charlotte regained her composure and picked the phone back up. "Did you say you are Hope, my son?" she asked the caller.

"Yes, Mom. This is your son, Hope. I am in town with my wife and son," he replied.

"Hope, my son—Hope, my son, is that really you? I have longed for you," she said as she broke down in tears.

"Who was that? Did I hear you say Hope?" asked Beverly.

"Yes, that is Hope, He is at a hotel downtown with his family," responded Charlotte.

"Girl, give me the phone. Let me talk to him."

"Just a minute. This is a special moment. I must be dreaming."

"Mom," Hope then said, "I would like to bring my family home this afternoon or tomorrow if you are available."

"Son, I want to see you and your family right now," she responded anxiously.

"My wife's name is Floretta. We named our son after Dad. He is Edmund II. Just so that you will know."

"Beverly, Hope is bringing his family home to see me," said Charlotte. "Stick around. You are family. You always have been and always will be part of our family."

"This is a miracle. I cannot wait to see my boy," added Beverly.

"We will see you in a couple of hours, Mom," said Hope, as he hung up the phone.

Suddenly, it dawned on Floretta that she was about to meet her mother-in-law. She quickly got Edmund II dressed up first so that she could take her time to look her best.

Within a couple of hours, Hope and his family arrived at Charlotte's residence. He knocked on the front door. Charlotte opened the door and hugged her son. Beverly stood beside her and gave Hope and Floretta hugs as well. Charlotte picked up her grandson, Edmund II, and kissed him.

They took their seats in the family room, and Hope formally introduced Floretta to his mom and Beverly. Strong emotions blanketed the entire family room. Charlotte had aged a lot more than Hope expected, probably due to stress-related issues. Beverly was bespectacled. She had also aged and gained more weight than Hope imagined.

Hope gave general information about what brought him back to Avenice. He saved the details of his experiences from the time he left home and of the prospect of CHIG's potential ventures in Avenice for a later date. He asked about Jimmy.

"He is not doing so well, son. He is now at a nursing home and taking life day by day," Charlotte replied.

"I would like to see him before I leave. Would that be possible?" he asked.

"Not in his current condition," she responded. "He has lost quite a bit of weight. Some of his vital organs are failing. I would have to alert the staff at the nursing home to prepare him in advance before you see him."

"Okay, I will not press the issue. I hope I can get to see him on my next trip to Avenice."

"Hope is all we have," remarked Charlotte. "I have learned that nothing in life can be guaranteed by anyone. I pray that you get your wish. Life is so fickle, you know?"

"Yes, it is. I certainly would like to have the opportunity to have a heartfelt chat with him. I believe forgiveness would be in order, Mom."

"There is a time for every purpose under the heavens. I will certainly inform him about your wish to have a private conversation with him.

"By the way, there is a box that Edmund, your father, left. I had Jimmy move it to your room. It has been there ever since. I have periodically thought about opening it. Jimmy at one time wanted to get rid of it from this house. He did not find value in a box that belonged to a dead man. However, I stopped him from doing that. I told him it might contain things that might be useful to you or at least serve as memorabilia for you. However, each time that thought crept up in my mind, I never had the courage to do so.

"I hid the keys to that box inside a blue container in the attic. I do not think with my current knee problems I can climb back in there. If you get into the attic, you will find that container to the east of the hot water heater. Maybe you should get it now that you are here. I have longed for this day."

"I certainly would. I am curious to know the contents of that box," replied Hope. He got up at once and climbed into the attic, where he successfully retrieved the keys. Edmund II fell asleep in his grandmother's arms while Floretta chatted with both Charlotte and Beverly. Hope opened the box in his room. He found several pictures of his ancestors.

However, the bulk of its contents included documents B.T. had passed on to Edmund. They included minutes of the family meetings, the De Pinto family tree, B.T.'s last will and testament, the original and modified versions of the conservation easement, and charitable donations by the De Pinto family.

In a separate folder, Hope saw a written testimony by two missionaries from a far country. B.T. on behalf of the De Pinto family had donated a parcel of land to two missionaries named Elisha Zimmermann and his brother Joseph Anderson. That parcel of land donation was later followed by monetary and other material assistance.

The parcel was intended to serve as a staging area for evangelistic work in Avenice and other parts of the state. The testimonial also noted that two indigenous men from GC helped the missionaries to translate their literary work into other languages under the shade of a huge oak tree.

Intuitively, Hope concluded that the vacant real property adjacent to the referenced site in the testimonial could serve as the location for CHIG's potential plant. He further thought that *GC* in the testimonial referred to Giboad City.

He additionally surmised that the two natives who assisted the missionaries either were blessed by the missionaries or adopted their names and eventually passed them on to Elisha Zimmermann, CHIG's board chairman, and Dr. Anderson. That explained the symbols on the rings they wore.

This memorable reunion between Hope and his mother was well worth it. It was hard for them to say goodbye to each other. He asked Charlotte to contract the services of a local repair person for the necessary repairs and maintenance of their family home. He offered to foot the cost of repairs.

Furthermore, Hope promised to stay in touch with both Charlotte and Beverly. He asked Charlotte if he could take the box with him, promising to return it at a future date.

Charlotte agreed to Hope's request. As they left the De Pinto residence, Beverly observed the birthmark on Floretta's eyelid but kept it to herself.

The following Monday morning Hope had his scheduled follow-up meeting with representatives of the consulting company he hired to do the comprehensive Environmental Impact Statement and subsequent work.

The consulting company prepared a brief report, marked "Private & Confidential," for Hope. It outlined the procedures they followed including the analysis and sound interpretation of data acquired. It substantiated Hope's suspicion that gold might be found within the western fringes of Avenice.

They swore to keep that information to themselves until Hope met with the local government officials in his capacity as successor in interest of the De Pinto family.

In a later emotionally charged meeting with the local government officials of Avenice, Hope skillfully built a case for modifying or terminating the conservation easement for portions of the western fringes of Avenice in contravention of its stated purpose.

The economic decline of the city had reached serious proportions that required drastic intervention. He referenced and invoked his grandfather's amendment to the easement. The entire De Pinto family attested to it. That meant they could simply agree with him, as landowner/successor in interest, with no need of court approval.

He provided the original and amended copies of the conservation easements for their consideration. He informed them that he needed that modification or termination in order to convince the board of CHIG to select Avenice as a prime location for CHIG's expansion that would revitalize the economy of Avenice.

After careful deliberation and review of the presented documents, the mayor and city council agreed with Hope's proposal for Avenice to receive substantial monetary compensations for portions of the western fringes of the city, for which the easement was lifted. Additionally, Avenice would receive tax revenues, creation of many jobs, and incidental financial rewards.

In light of such strong accomplishments, Hope again gave a solid presentation to CHIG's board of directors confirming the points he had previously noted in favor of selecting Avenice as a prime location and the Environmental Impact Statement. He noted that the conservation easement protecting parts of the western fringes of Avenice was no longer an issue. He received a standing ovation for his superb and creative leadership and business development efforts.

The board approved Hope's proposal. It was no longer a figment of his imagination or a dream. It became reality. Within weeks, CHIG scheduled construction activities to begin.

CHAPTER 18

The Joy of Success

News of CHIG's business development ventures spread like wildfire in both Giboad City and Avenice. Hope organized a well-publicized press conference to inform the public of CHIG's ventures in Avenice. Initially, CHIG would build a very large computer manufacturing plant, which would employ several thousand people.

Later, a massive pharmaceutical complex that would manufacture drugs to meet both local and international markets would follow the computer plant. Furthermore, he revealed the involvement of TENA University in CHIG's ventures at Avenice through a memorandum of agreement.

Within weeks, groundbreaking activities for the construction of CHIG's plant at Avenice commenced. A large fence was constructed to protect the light and heavy equipment and machinery to be used in construction. Mobile trailers were brought in to be used as temporary offices. Here and there at the site, several workers could be seen wearing hard hats.

Two of the mobile trailers served as employment offices. The human resources department at CHIG was renamed Talent Engagement Services. It continued to hire and train new employees in some of the mobile trailers or in out-of-use conference halls.

Construction of the new facilities was scheduled to be completed ahead of time since most of the structures were prefabricated. Within weeks, Avenice gradually took on the characteristics of a city that was bouncing back from economic decadence.

People heard about the ongoing employment opportunities. Many people who had left the city due to lack of employment gradually returned home to Avenice, including Angie and her dad. Within months, housing construction also began. Housing units sold like hotcakes. As quickly as they could be completed, people were buying and moving into them.

Fast food restaurants as well as formal restaurants sprang up all over the town. The impact of the new construction on Avenice was great. New infrastructure was put in place. There was a need for more schools, law enforcement officers, city workers.

While those activities went on, Hope bought a three-acre plot of land on the outskirts of town to build a house for his family. They built their house on a lot that overlooked a nearby sparkling lake. Floretta had already picked the type of furniture she wanted in their home. She wanted everything set up immaculately before she invited her parents over for the weekend.

She adopted two dogs for Edmund II. She named them Neptune and Beau. The startup activities at the plant kept Hope very busy. He was preoccupied with meetings throughout the week. In turn, Floretta kept herself very busy at home. She made time to meet the needs of her husband. Furthermore, she directed the housekeeper to keep their house immaculately clean, pleasant, and orderly.

Hope promised they would go on a brief family vacation once construction of the computer production plant was completed. CHIG had additional expansion projects on the drawing board at Avarice. They included a pharmaceutical plant and one other project he did not elaborate on to her.

Though he was preoccupied with the ongoing work at Avenice, Hope made time for Charlotte, his mother. They invited her to stay with them as Edmund II's nanny. However, she desired to remain in their family house and visit them periodically, especially during the weekends.

Hope kept his promise to have their family home where he grew up remodeled. The landscaping of her front and back yards were also restored. With the help of Beverly, the garden that Edmund used to plant was rejuvenated. Once again, it thrived with a variety of vegetables as it once did. Since Charlotte lived alone in her house, Hope had the most recent available electronic surveillance systems installed to monitor her house.

Eventually, the first phase of CHIG's business development ventures, the computer production plant, was fully completed. It went into full operation with the ability to meet both local and international demands. The plant exceeded projections for return on investment for CHIG.

Hope remembered the value and friendship of his childhood friend, Angie, and her father to Charlotte and himself. He arranged to have Angie's father hired in a supervisory role at the computer production plant.

Within a few weeks, Phase 2 of CHIG's expansion in Avenice, which entailed the construction of a pharmaceutical production plant, would commence. Hope fulfilled his promise to take his wife and son on a family vacation before that process began.

Hope wanted this vacation to be unique. Thus, he took his family to a place known to be the birthplace of his faith. They arrived and checked into their hotel, which was located along the shores of a very large lake. They noticed that most of the vacationers who stayed at that hotel were there for reasons other than rest, relaxation, and enjoyment of scenic beauty.

The salt and other mineral composition of its water was several times higher than that of the seas or oceans. The density of the waters of that lake was also much higher than that of pure water. It was dense enough for swimmers to float without flotation devices.

Because of its unique chemical composition, it healed a variety of dermatological ailments on people who bathed in it. The lake was so clear that one could see salt crystals that looked like gravel several feet deep to the bottom of it.

The day after their arrival, they got on a tour bus. They travelled to a holy site that contained remnants of a huge edifice that used to be a temple. That reminded him of the incomplete and abandoned place of worship adjacent to the site he had chosen for CHIG's plant in Avenice.

The following day, another tour bus took them to the actual birthplace of the originator of his faith, Yeshua of Nazareth, and then to a high mountain identified as the Mount of Transfiguration.

Later in the afternoon, they stopped over at a couple of sites where written records existed for supernatural miracles performed by Yeshua. Hope had a handwritten prayer and supplication in his pocket. He solemnly included his petitions previously in his sanctum at home. Something had prompted him to write them down and take them along on this trip. Over the years, Hope had learned to follow that inner voice deep within him. He stuck that handwritten prayer request into one of the shrubs that adorned the monastery at that tourist site.

On their way back to the hotel, the tour bus made one last stop for the day. They visited a community of people who lived in isolation from what some might consider the real world. They had a unique lifestyle. Their outlook on life was to invest trust in the real promise of a positive outcome. They did not stress over anything. Neither did they have any health issues. They believed there was no problem completely new to humankind. All issues we face in life's journey have afflicted others before. However, those that have hope of a positive outcome rose above such challenges.

They believed without a doubt that those who have hope are endowed with a guiding light within that shows them how to navigate through life's problems. Thus, the awareness of hope serves as a global positioning system that both motivates and navigates humankind through difficult times. The awareness of hope cultivates self-confidence.

Embedded within these people was a supernatural force that impressed solutions of trials on their mind, virtually causing them to draw upon their vocabulary to articulate what must be done to get out of one's predicament. In their thinking, to lose hope is to give up on any potential for experiencing a better tomorrow. Those who fall prey to that are likely to usher in negative thoughts that enable bad spirits to enter and torment humankind.

Furthermore, they were convinced that all humans have a desire to hear good rather than dismal and negative news, which makes it much easier to win over people on the side of positivity. Hope thought about his life and could identify with the outlook of life of those people.

Hope and his family rested in their hotel for a few days. They next toured other nearby sites of interest. Finally, they visited the places of the death and resurrection of Yeshua. They concluded their vacation and returned home to Avenice with many souvenirs.

One Saturday afternoon after they returned from their lengthy vacation abroad, Hope invited Jimmy to their new house. Such a visit required that Jimmy must be accompanied by a nurse practitioner because of his numerous and complex health issues.

Charlotte made those arrangements with Jimmy's healthcare provider. On the day of their arrival, the health care provider wheeled Jimmy into Hope's elegant house. He could not help but admire its grandeur. Jimmy looked at Hope in a very sorrowful way during their conversations. He admitted it was never in his wildest dream that he would witness Hope's awesome accomplishments.

Hope was aware that Jimmy's doctors gave him only a few months to live. He also sensed that Jimmy's conscience bothered him regarding the evil things he had craftily planned and executed against Hope, which led Hope to leave home. He was courageous enough to ask for forgiveness from Hope.

Hope gave Jimmy a bear hug and forgave him. They cried on each other's shoulders. After that emotional encounter, Jimmy's nurse drove him back to the nursing home. That would be his permanent home.

Floretta brought with her all the poems and color paintings she had received from Hope during their courtship in Giboad City. She valued them highly. She chose three of his poems and one that she wrote to him and had them custom-framed.

She displayed them prominently in one of their upstairs entertainment rooms so that she could admire their meaning and essence every day. She read them one by one:

Unto Thee I Grant

If I had the power to give health
Or the power to give long life,
If I had power over wealth
Or power over happiness,
Unto thee I grant.
If I had power over success
Or power over sorrow,
If I had power over pain
Or power for a better tomorrow,
Unto thee I grant.
In you I find no fault;
With you, I feel secured,
More secured than money in a vault.
However, none of these do I have.
Take heart, there is no need to fear,
Nor is there a reason to be afraid.
For there's one thing I know I have:
It is love unlimited,
And that to thee I grant.

To My Love

Come with me under the oak tree,
For there we will be able to enjoy
The cool breeze of being free.
Gladly will I show you how to heal
The ailment of a broken heart,
True Love knows no bounds,

However, unfaithfulness pierces like a dart,
To trace my love you need no bounds;
To be devoted to you is my promise to you.
Nevertheless, remember it is a two-way street,
Whatever it is you expect of me.
There is never a day without you on my mind;
Another you I will never find.
My love for you will never fade.
Under the shade, we will have it made.
It is not your pride;
Else, from you I will forever hide.
It is not your money, nor your looks;
On me you can put no hooks.
It is not your clothes, not your car;
Several with you will be at par.
It is an unchanging feeling I have for you,
And this is my concept of love.

On Life

There is no need to fear.
Neither is there a reason to cry.
I have no doubts, my dear,
That my love for you will never run dry.
Nor is there reason to despair.
Some may come, and some may go;
However, with you I will always remain.
Those who lift you high
May be the same to bring you down.
Life is like a mirror;

Handle it with caution;
Wipe it clean; keep it safe.
Once broken, cannot be replaced.

To Hope

Hope, my love—Hope, my love,
You are mightier than the Ocean.
Hope, my love—Hope, my love,
My love for you is not just a notion.
Never in life, could there be so much devotion.
As long as into the Ocean the rivers flow,
So forever, our love will grow.
I have heard of kings;
I have heard of princes;
I have heard of sheiks;
I have heard of riches.
However, none my love would I give.
You are mightier than a king is.
Your unchanging love is like a sieve;
It separates the real from unreal in me.
Your breath is like a cool breeze;
Your lips are sweeter than honey from a bee.
With you I will never freeze;
The future I always will see.
In unity, our love will grow mightier.
The tides of love will it overcome
Until thy kingdom come.

Several preconstruction-planning meetings were held in the large conference room of the computer production plant. Hope was at the helm of those meetings. The news media covered the groundbreaking ceremonies.

Ultimately, construction of the pharmaceutical production complex began. Hiring of potential employees commenced. Hope was aware that his childhood friend, Angie, was a trained pharmacologist. Once again, he recommended her as a potential candidate for employment when pharmaceutical production operations began.

Hope received a lot of publicity locally and out of town. There was always some type of news coverage on the new projects at Avenice, which he spearheaded. He additionally got exposure in the local newspapers. A TV talk show host featured him on the *Prime Time Live* show. Many in the viewing area watched that show. He became an overnight celebrity.

Rankings of the top ten places to live and raise a family in listed Avenice at number one. The once economically destitute city became a beacon of hope in the entire state. However, there were more good things to share about Avenice.

Negotiations took place between CHIG, led by Hope, and the local city government for a Phase 3 project. It was a gold mining operation. It would be located at the western boundary of Avenice. Certainly, that caught the general population off guard. They were unaware of the investigative work for minerals at the western boundaries of Avenice Hope initiated with the environmental consulting firm.

Their report was closely guarded until now. The landowner, the De Pinto family, City of Avenice, and CHIG would jointly own the mining company. Profits from that venture for the De Pinto family and City of Avenice would be used for developing additional infrastructure, building schools and hospitals, and improving the quality of life for the citizens of Avenice.

Hope retained the environmental consulting firm for that project, as well. There was evidence of alluvial deposits of gold nuggets at the western fringes of Avenice. However, due to the existence of the conservation easement, no one had paid any attention to prospect it for gold.

The existence of quartz crystals was included in the environmental report prepared by the consulting firm, which boosted confidence in proven gold reserves at the study area. Metal detectors were also used to scan the area, and results confirmed the existence of gold on the site.

In advance of formal mining activities, the prospective operators of the facility claimed the mining site. Contacts were duly made with applicable state and federal government agencies to verify the existence of a previous claim of the site.

Certainly, the original conservation easement eliminated that possibility. The plan for the mining development was to begin on a smaller scale and then expand the operation.

Hope's consultants advocated collaboration with advocacy organizations and preparation of housing for the mineworkers and electric power supply. In order to mini-mize impacts to the operational area, solar and wind energy resources were considered. Plans were put in place for profes-sional excavation, setup and storage, as well as packaging of the product.

Hope at Last

Amid all the great things that took place in Avenice, mostly initiated by Hope, he remained humble. He did not publicly take credit for them. Hope believed in teamwork. He was convinced that a lot more could be accomplished if they worked together. He was a strong advocate of the power of hope and diversity at all dimensions of humanity's well-being. He also felt strongly that there was unity in diversity.

Hope kept his heart and hands clean from controversy. He maintained a positive attitude and smiled so much under various circumstances that people outside his realm of influence thought he never had problems of any kind. He was a charismatic person. People enjoyed being in his company.

Another dramatic event took place at CHIG. Elisha Zimmermann retired from active work. He stepped down as board chairman for CHIG. He pulled all the necessary strings to turn his role over to Hope.

Due to a number of favorable investment conditions in Avenice, including business tax breaks and free trade zones, CHIG made a business decision to relocate its corporate headquarters from Giboad City to Avenice.

Hope took stock of the massive industrial complex units he managed. With the thousands of employees he employed, he felt the need to recruit someone to oversee security operations. He wanted someone he could trust. Someone who valued loyalty. Someone whom he could depend on.

The name of one person flashed in his mind. He picked up his phone and made a call to Giboad City. "Hello, may I speak to Quincy?" he said.

"Speaking. May I know who is calling?"

"Your long-lost friend Hope—Hope De Pinto?"

"Well, well, well," Quincy replied. "What did I do to receive a call from a superstar like you today? We have been reading and hearing about your unimaginable accomplishments in Avenice. I saw Tina the other day. They are in the process of relocating to Avenice."

"Great, one good deed deserves another," Hope responded. "We are looking forward to their stay in Avenice."

"You still have not told me the reason for your call."

"Yes, I wanted to invite you to my office in Avenice for a very private discussion."

"Really?"

"Yes, really," Hope said. :Will you be able to fly down here this coming Friday, all expenses on me?"

"Perfect, I'm off this Friday. That will work well for me. May I know what I'm coming down there for?"

"You will find out when you get here. It is a surprise. By the way, would it be possible to you to find out the name and contact information for the train driver the day I first met you at that station?"

"Well, sir, it has been a while," Quincy replied. But I will do my best to get that information for you."

"That will be most appreciated. So sorry to connect with you on short notice. I really appreciate it. Bye for now," said Hope.

"Bye. See you on Friday."

On Friday morning at nine, Hope's administrative assistant buzzed to inform him Quincy waited in the reception area. Hope asked her to bring him to his office.

"Welcome to Avenice. How was your flight? Is everything okay at your hotel?" inquired Hope.

"It's all good. I feel very fortunate to be here."

"I invited you here because I thought about you, and wanted to return a favor."

"Return a favor?" Quincy asked.

"Yes. You were the one who opened the door for me to meet with Tina unexpectedly. There must have been a reason for that. Things like that do not happen by accident. Of course, the rest of the story is history. I want to ask you for a favor."

"You don't owe me anything. You needed help genuinely, and I did what I thought I should do for you. I happened to be at the right place at the right time."

"That's what I'm talking about," responded Hope: "being in the right place at the right time. One good deed deserves another. I will have an opening for our head of security here. I could not think of a better person for that position than you. Regardless of my current position, I consider you a friend. If I could interest you in taking that position, you will make me a very happy friend indeed.

"You are not happy with the system you have right now?"

"We are following the same pattern as in Giboad City. I don't just need warm bodies here. I need a certain level of comfort with my security person in light of the things we are doing. I can see in your eyes that you have what we need. Would you take that position if it was offered to you?"

"I most certainly would," Quincy answered. "I guess I can say that I have been looking for an opportunity to grow in my job. This will be more like it. In addition, when you asked me for information on the train driver I took it upon myself to investigate him a little further. I came across some information that might interest you. He has close ties in Avenice. He fathered a son called Jimmy, who I understand is hospitalized."

"You mean that train driver is Jimmy's biological father?" asked Hope.

"Yes. I also learned that he was abusive to both Jimmy and his mother. He has turned a new leaf. I mean, he cleaned up his act, and is looking forward to retirement."

"I can't believe that. The train driver was part of the divine plan of my destiny. That is very interesting. Maybe he can work here in our transportation department part-time if he needs a job."

"I have his contact information. Here it is," Quincy said.

"I appreciate that. I will tell Tina about our conversation later today. She will know what to do to make things happen. Have a safe trip back. Hope to see you here soon. Thanks again," said Hope, as he ended his interview with Quincy.

After Quincy's return to Giboad City, Hope called Tina. He informed her about his conversation with Quincy, and asked her to follow up with Quincy to ensure that he gets the position as head of security at CHIG's industrial complex in Avenice.

At the scheduled time, Tina and her talent engagement staff relocated to Avenice. They admired the more spacious and modern facilities at CHIG's brand new corporate offices in Avenice.

Things moved along smoothly as expected in all the three phases of business development projects masterminded by Hope. All the employees were trained in CHIG's standard operating procedures (SOP). They were comfortable with their assigned duties. No major accidents occurred that disrupted normal operations at all three industrial sites.

After all the hard work that went into the planning, construction, start-up, and smooth operations of the new industrial complex units at Avenice, Hope threw a huge party at his residence. He invited family and friends who helped him through it all. The guest list included Charlotte and Beverly. Jimmy's health issues did not allow him to attend; however, his dad, Kevin, took his place. Dr. Anderson and Elisha Zimmermann attended, as well as Tina Doyer, Barry and Irene Pritchard, Quincy Baah, Angie and her dad, Beula and Estella, and Alvin, president of the environmental consulting firm that produced the Environmental Impact Statement for Hope.

Everyone had a great time at the party. Hope announced he had an agreement with the mayor of Avenice to rename one of the city parks in honor of his late childhood friend and confidant, Roger.

Hope noticed that his mother whispered into Beverly's ear when Tina was introduced at the gathering. While the catering company served meals amid soft music, Hope pulled Charlotte aside to the balcony to learn what she had whispered to Beverly. "Are you having a good time, Mom?" he asked.

"Yes, everything has turned out great. I am really proud of you, my son."

"Did I live up to the expectations of you and Dad?"

"Certainly, this is a dream come true," she said. "It demonstrates that while we all have plans in life, life itself also has its own plans for us. When we were born, we had our destiny embedded in us. Our challenge is to synchronize what we seek for ourselves, with what life has prepared for us. You are a true testament of that. Just look at what we all went through, especially you. At the end, all things work together for our good to manifest His will for you, no matter how hard others tried to derail your purpose."

"But, Mom, I saw a certain look on your face when Tina was introduced. She was the one who hired me at CHIG under mysterious circumstances, you know. I was just curious to know what you whispered to Beverly."

"I had a flashback when she was introduced. It was several years ago, way back before you were born. I did not know a moment like this would present itself for me to go back in time. I remember Tina. She would have been your mom instead of me."

"Tina would have been my mom instead of you?" he asked. "How could that be?"

"I remember that walk, and her smile. I remember her dimples and freckles. We were very young and single, in our teenage years. She was very hurt when her relationship with Edmund did not work out the way she wanted. Meanwhile, your dad was introduced to me. He wanted me pregnant quickly. I think Tina was barren. That was why Edmund's family did not approve of her. However, I do not know that for sure, and Edmund did not discuss that with me when he found out I knew about his prior relationship with Tina. She loved him very much. Edmund did tell me Tina told him that she wished an opportunity would come to repay him for the way he had treated her during their relationship. And so I guess her wish eventually came to pass."

"Oh, Mom, you may be right. During my interview with her at CHIG, she made brief statements that led me to believe she knew Dad. However, we never got the chance to elaborate. She has been of great help. Nevertheless, I am proud of you as my mom. Nothing and no one can replace you. I promise," he assured her.

"So now you know, son."

"Yes, I do. Let us get back in with the other guests." He took her arm, and the two of them walked back in to join the party.

Hope found Floretta engaged in a conversation with Beverly. Edmund II sat beside Floretta.

"I'm glad you came, Beverly," said Hope. "You have been supportive of Charlotte and me. We consider you family. You always will be. I hope you shared some of my childhood stories with Floretta."

"Yes, we hit it right off. I was telling your wife how pleasant you have always been and what a good man you are. You have taken on the looks of your dad, Edmund. Your son was rightly named after him. He too will grow up one of these days and follow your example.

"Hope, do not let me forget to tell you how beautiful your wife is. When you stopped by Charlotte's house the other time, things were so hectic, I did not get the chance to visit with your family, as I should. I am glad this opportunity arose to give us a second chance to get to know each other better."

"Of course, the pleasure is all ours. Do not be a stranger. Anytime you desire to stop by our doors are always open to you."

"I will," said Beverly. "You will be seeing me around more often. You can count on that."

"You know, Aunt Beverly, all these years that I have known you, I never paid attention to the birthmark you have on your left eyelid. I see that both Floretta and Edmund II have similar birthmarks on their left eyelids. That must be a coincidence," remarked Hope.

"I'm glad you brought that up. I noticed that the very first time I met your wife, but as I said things happened so abruptly when you first came by your mom's house the other day. Sounds like we need to pursue that later, huh?"

"Sure we will. We must. Very interesting," said Hope as he walked off to mingle with the other guests.

At the close of the party, Hope made one final announcement that came as a shock to many. He revealed that negotiations were ongoing for CHIG to acquire Senecan Manufacturing Company, where his father-in-law, Barry, worked as supervisor. When that acquisition took place, he intended to promote Barry to plant manager.

Hope thanked his guests for attending the party. One by one, they left for their respective destinations.

Hope's accomplishments for the city of Avenice and the De Pinto family spread across the state like wildfire. Those who drove through Avenice prior to the growth of the industrial complexes that revived the economy of that city could not believe the transformation that had taken place. The city was livelier than during its heyday. It was estimated that about 4200 new families were moving into Avenice monthly.

It had gone from a bust to a boom city because of Hope's visions and actions—the dreams of his parents, as well as his own desires to be the channel through whom revival of the economy, and the prestige of Avenice and his family, became reality. He received lots of publicity from all aspects of the news media. Nevertheless, his desires and aspirations continued to unfold even more fully than anyone else imagined. He was not completely satisfied with his accomplishment.

He wanted to get out of his comfort zone and reach for the moon. Somewhere he heard that the average human only used about 10–15 percent of his or her capabilities. The remainder was unused and taken to the grave. He made it a point to rise above that statistic. Yes, he was determined to reach for the moon and beyond.

One Saturday morning he sat in a reclining chair on an upstairs balcony, watching the glitter of the morning sun over the clear blue waters of the lake only a few yards away from his house. Hope mused over his future. He breathed the air of spiritual maturity. He recalled all the challenges he had gone through and how providence, persistence, or perseverance synchronized with divine favor worked behind the scenes in his favor to get him to the heights he had attained thus far.

He had a secret formula he put into practice and followed rigorously. He was an enlightened spiritual man who understood the power of prayer. This was his prayer secret. It worked for him. He believed that certain dynamics must be followed for an effective prayer to be promptly answered. The prayer dynamics that must be pursued when we ask, seek, or knock on the heavenly gates must be rooted in deep faith in God. One must have a will to transform one's belief into reality. It is not enough to have faith in faith; one's faith must be in the living God. God must be the object of that faith, period.

Secondly, one must understand that the purpose of prayer is to remove the obstacles, no matter how big they may be, that the enemy has placed on our spiritual path.

There is a type of faith that one develops through hearing the word of God and then standing on those words in prayer. Nevertheless, there is another type of faith that the Holy Spirit imparts on those who believe in Yeshua. One must not doubt the uttered words of one's prayer. Furthermore, one must desire and expect what was asked in prayer.

Finally, we must forgive those who have wronged us at the time we render our prayer. Hope considered the above process as the core of "the dynamism of a will and way to win." That was his prayer secret. That was his formula for success.

Based on his accomplishments thus far with the application of that formula, he entertained the idea of running for governor of his state. He prayed about it together with Floretta. He felt deep within his spirit that he was destined for success, based on faith in God, who had been with him and never forsaken him in all his trials and tribulations. He had no prior political experience. He was not a political science major. Neither did he have a political base. All he had was the dynamism of a will and way to win.

Hope discussed his political aspirations with Elisha and Dr. Anderson. They assured him that they would do all they could to help him succeed. He delegated certain aspects of his work to trusted members of his professional team so that he could run as a gubernatorial candidate. He hired political consultants. Dr. Anderson arranged to have the political science department at TENA University conduct polls. Elisha contacted the numerous friends he had in the business community to buy in to Hope's campaign with significant monetary and other material contributions.

Soon, Hope's campaign strategy was formulated. His campaign team decided to mount an all-out grassroots political campaign that employed among other strategies the following elements:

1. Buy time slots for TV advertisements;
2. Train and use volunteers for door-to-door canvassing;

3. Train and use volunteers for street canvassing.
4. Train and use professionals as well as volunteers in phone banking.
5. Train and use volunteers for tabling at events.
6. Identify supporters who were willing and able to organize house parties.
7. Organize personal appearances and educational events.
8. Train and use both professionals and volunteers in social media campaigns and texting.

Hope had already received much-needed exposure from the media, including television networks, radio, and newspaper and other publications because of the phenomenal work he did to revive Avenice from its economic doldrums to the status of one of the most favored cities to live and raise a family. He had a most favorable record of accomplishment in addition to his charisma and sound finances, name recognition, business connections, and most of all his faith in God.

His political strategists organized him to make appearances at key cities and venues. On one such appearance, a new reporter asked him his stand on the death penalty. Hope said he believed in the criminal justice system. However, he was opposed to the death penalty. Many people who heard about his accomplishments wanted to meet him personally. He was eloquent and enjoyed a stable marriage. No one could dig up any skeletons in his social or business life. Polls showed he led his rivals by double-digit percentages.

Election Day arrived. Voter turnout was heavy. Polls indicated that Hope would win by a landslide. That is the way it was. The state had a brand-new, youthful, and charismatic governor with an ability to get things done. Some even wondered whether Hope should consider a run for the presidency. However, he wanted to do one thing at a time.

A scheduled execution of an inmate who had been on death row for many years fell on the day after Hope became governor. The media did a good job to publicize that execution and replayed the interview Hope had given about his opposition to the death penalty.

All eyes were on Hope to see whether he would practice what he preached. The execution was to take place at midnight. If the governor granted no pardon, then it would go forward as planned.

Exhausted from the intense political campaign and celebrations, Hope took a nap. There were anxious moments as the midnight hour approached. Floretta woke him up late in the evening. Hope found a note he made to call and grant a pardon to that inmate.

The prisoner, whose real name was changed in prison to Eli Okoe, was already strapped to the execution table. Witnesses to the execution were already seated. The warden kept on looking at the clock on the wall as midnight approached. Everyone was convinced that Eli Okoe would be executed at midnight.

Then at long last Hope, the newly sworn governor, called in for a stay of execution. He gave that prisoner a second chance for life. During the last few years of his life in prison, Eli reformed. He voraciously studied the Bible and took classes in biblical studies. He earned a divinity degree while in prison.

Upon his pardon and subsequent release from prison, Eli was moved into a halfway house to ensure his transition to society was uneventful. He was interviewed by several television stations about his experiences in prison and the moments immediately prior to the governor's call to grant a stay of execution. Finally, the television reporter asked Eli to state two wishes he had on his heart.

Barry and Irene were in Avenice for the weekend. They stayed with Hope and Floretta. They enjoyed the company of Edmund II as well. Privately, Barry was there to work out details of his new position as plant manager at Senecan Manufacturing. Incidentally, both Charlotte and Beverly also were at Hope's residence because the Pritchards were in town. They all caught glimpses of Eli's interview on TV.

Eli's response was startling. He answered the questions articulately. He stated that he was afflicted with a terminal illness. Nevertheless, the two wishes on his heart were, first, to pastor a local church before his time to depart life on earth caught up with him. Second, he narrated certain incidents that took place in his business career he regretted. They ultimately landed him in prison and cost him his marriage and relationship with a daughter he never knew. Those would make his second chance of life well worth it.

Charlotte turned and looked at a sobbing Beverly dead in the eyes. She recalled the story Beverly told her about her previous life after they watched the movie Kiddie's Baby and said, "Beverly, oh Beverly, that's you he is talking about. I think you must go back to your first love."

"I know. It is all coming back to me now. But how would I answer the question about his daughter I gave up for adoption?" asked Beverly.

Hope was obviously moved by Eli's appeal. He committed to helping him raise funds to complete the worship center located at the western fringes of Avenice with the huge oak tree in front of it. This was the original sanctuary that the two missionaries, Zimmermann and Anderson, could not complete for Eli.

At that point, Hope looked at Floretta and Edmund II, especially at the birthmark on their left eyelids. Barry and Irene raised their eyebrows when they heard the term *adoption*. However, no one said anything further about the matter.

Hope went into his Sanctum to meditate. The spiritual visitations he had whenever he was at the crossroads of a major decision strengthened him to keep his eyes on the hope of Yeshua of Nazareth. Alone in his sanctum, Hope slowly and pensively read the following verses in the Holy Bible:

> Be of good courage, and he shall strengthen your heart, all ye that hope in the LORD. (Psalm 31:24)

> Behold, the eye of the LORD is upon them that fear him, upon them that hope in his mercy. (Psalm 33:18)

> And now, LORD, what wait I for? my hope is in thee. (Psalm 39:7)

> Why art thou cast down, O my soul? and why art thou disquieted within me? hope thou in God: for I shall yet praise him, who is the health of my countenance, and my God. (Psalm 42:11)

> For thou art my hope, O Lord GOD: thou art my trust from my youth. (Psalm 75:5)

> Happy is he that hath the God of Jacob
> for his help, whose hope is in the Lord
> his God. (Psalm 146:5)

Thus saith the Lord; Cursed be the man that trusteth in man, and maketh flesh his arm, and whose heart departeth from the Lord.

For he shall be like the heath in the desert, and shall not see when good cometh; but shall inhabit the parched places in the wilderness, in a salt land and not inhabited.

Blessed is the man that trusteth in the Lord, and whose hope the Lord is.

For he shall be as a tree planted by the waters, and that spreadeth out her roots by the river, and shall not see when heat cometh, but her leaf shall be green; and shall not be careful in the year of drought, neither shall cease from yielding fruit. (Jeremiah 17:5–8)

Suddenly, Hope fell into a trance. In that state, he saw an image of the silver coin, which his father, Edmund, presented to him in a prior vision. A blue ribbon was tied around the silver coin. Hope then realized that the figure who presented him with the silver coin was not his late dad, Edmund. It was Yeshua of Nazareth Himself who presented him with the medallion. In fact, Yeshua had been that driving force that appeared to him on previous occasions. However, in order not to frighten Hope, he assumed the appearance of someone Hope knew and was comfortable with. That was his late father.

For the first time, Hope actually heard Yeshua's voice. He said, *"I am your hope!"*

I AM YOUR HOPE